MW01284328

The Fibonacci Murders

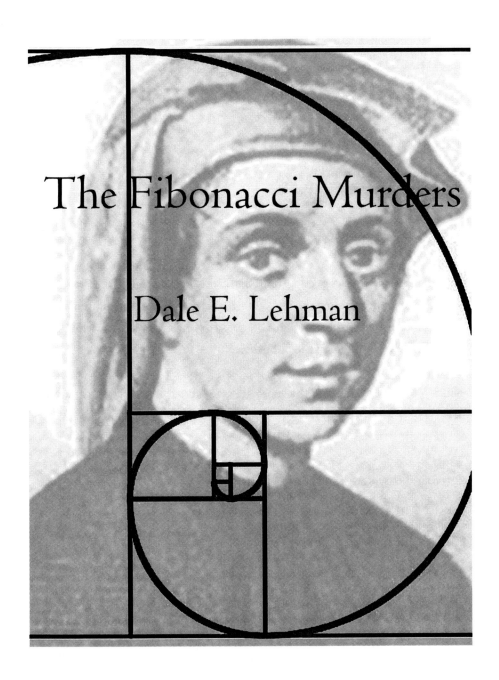

The Fibonacci Murders

Dale E. Lehman

SERPENT CLIFF

The Fibonacci Murders
Dale E. Lehman

Copyright © 2014 by Dale E. Lehman

All rights reserved. Except as permitted under U.S. Copyright Act of 1976, no
part of this publication may be reproduced, distributed, or transmitted in any
form or by any means, or stored in a database or retrieval system, without the
prior written permission of the publisher.

This is a work of fiction. All the characters, organizations, and events portrayed
in this book are either products of the author's imagination or are used
fictitiously.

Cover design by Kathleen Lehman

Published by Serpent Cliff, an imprint of One Voice Press, LLC
Essex, Maryland
www.onevoicepress.com

ISBN: 978-1-940135-25-0

Printed in the United States of America by Gasch Printing, Odenton, Maryland.

First Edition: October 2014
10 9 8 7 6 5 4 3 2 1

For Kathleen, my wife, best friend, and personal editor, without whom I would never have written anything publishable.

ACKNOWLEDGMENTS

Many people came together to bring this book from imagination to publication. Foremost is my editor and wife, Kathleen Lehman, who saved me from an embarrassment of errors and worked hard to put a shine on the finished product. She probably deserves a byline! I am also grateful to our Canadian friends David and Belinda Erickson, who read and commented on an early version of the manuscript. Special mention is due to my daughter and editorial assistant Jocelyn Lehman, who not only is Kathleen's right arm on the business front but is the one who keeps the household from falling apart. I should also mention my son Geoffrey, who keeps our spirits up by reminding us that no matter wnat the calendar says, Halloween is always just around the corner. Finally, over sixty friends, family members, and total strangers contributed to a Kickstarter project for this book. Every one of them has my deepest gratitude. The following people collectively contributed nearly half of the total and deserve special recognition as patrons of this book:

Bill, Andrea, and Bridget Bullock
Elizabeth and Joe Hamilton
Li-Su Javedan
Emmit and Juanita Lehman
Claire and Stewart Mathison
Melissa and Matthew Ward
with
Samara & Gabriel Greear and Rose Ward

Thank you one and all!

About the Setting

Those who live there know that Howard County, Maryland, is a real place and will no doubt recognize many of the names of towns, streets, parks, rivers and whatnot mentioned in the following tale. But I didn't take verisimilitude to extremes. Some details of the real world were changed to suit the story, while other setting elements were made up from whole cloth. I assure you, shoddy research didn't enter into it. At least not on that score. I won't guarantee perfection in all other areas . . .

Chapter I

First I must state two things: I am a mathematician, and I am not crazy. I mention the first because it alone explains my involvement in the events that recently took place in Howard County, Maryland. Otherwise, I would have had no connection to them whatsoever and would have been spared injury. I mention the second for two reasons. First: strangeness is associated in the public mind with my profession, notwithstanding that relatively few mathematicians are odder than the average person. Second: it seems to me the tale I'm about to tell could only have been imagined by a lunatic. Indeed, there was a lunatic. But he was not I.

With those points in mind, let us proceed.

Mathematical studies typically begin with a question or curious observation. In this case, it began with both. Σ

The envelope had landed on top of a pile of paperwork, to the casual glance one snowflake in a storm. Snowflakes are supposed to be unique, Detective Lieutenant Rick Peller thought as he eyed it. But if you don't look closely you don't notice the differences, and who looks closely in a blizzard?

Snow was on Peller's mind just then. It lay sixteen inches deep and counting on the ground outside Northern District Headquarters and, more to the point, on streets rendered impassable by the stuff. The whole of Maryland east of the mountains had flown into a panic as the late February storm trundled up from the south. Residents stripped grocery shelves of milk, bread, and toilet paper. Now few were out and about aside from TV reporters bundled up alongside impassable roads informing viewers how treacherous and, well, impassable those roads were. Stay home, they told the camera. Just stay home.

The mugger Criminal Investigations Division detectives had privately dubbed "the mad golfer" had apparently been following that advice. Not that he'd find any victims if he did try to play in the snow. A good thing, certainly, but with a downside: Peller wouldn't make any progress on the case today. They had little to go on aside from the location—all four attacks had occurred in or around Centennial Park—and the medical reports describing nearly identical wounds on the backs of the heads of the victims, who had been relieved of their money and jewelry. Only one victim remembered much of anything: the bloodied head of a Wilson nine-iron resting on the ground in front of his face while someone, squatting beside him like a pro lining up a putt, yanked his Omega watch from his wrist.

Well. There was no good way to get beat up, but at least nobody had died, and just maybe the victims would have a weird story to tell their grandkids someday.

Peller eyed the newly-arrived envelope without much interest. It couldn't possibly have a bloodstained golf club inside, at any rate. Neatly hand-lettered in a tight script, addressed to him personally, postmarked three days ago on Friday, February twenty-fifth in Cambridge on the Eastern Shore, it bore a return address he didn't recognize. Someplace called Leonardo's of Pisa. An Italian restaurant? Peller didn't care much for pasta. Having grown up in Lockport, New York, thirty miles northeast of Buffalo, he was principally a meat and potatoes man, although he had taken a liking to the Chesapeake region's specialty, the blue crab.

He took up the envelope and weighed it by feel. It was light, as though it only contained a single sheet of paper, and upon opening it he discovered he was right. The paper was folded into precise thirds, and in the same neat script as on the envelope it bore an odd message. Peller read it twice, feeling his mouth twist itself into a frown.

I start with zero. Nobody dies today.

"Hey Corina," he called over his shoulder. "Come have a look at this."

The slight, dark-haired woman gazing through the window at the falling snow pivoted on her heel. Thanks to the storm, she was one of only four detectives currently in the office. Peller smiled inwardly as she rushed to his side, swerving around unoccupied chairs and battered desks. The woman never did anything at a leisurely pace.

The scowl with which she had regarded the outside world remained fixed to her face as she approached, but Peller knew it wasn't for him. When she was fourteen, Corina Montufar had come with her family to the U.S. from Guatemala. Winter hadn't been part of her lexicon then, and even twenty-one years later, now a Detective Sergeant, she looked upon it as an unpleasant aberration.

"You found a golf club in the slush?" she asked, deadpan. Her accent was light—lighter, Peller thought, than it had been several years ago, as though she'd been consciously ridding herself of it.

"I wish." He nodded at the note now lying on his desk. "This came in the mail. Better not touch it without gloves."

She bent over the note for a minute. Finally, she shook her head. "I don't get it. Who tells the cops they *aren't* going to whack somebody?"

Peller pointed to the envelope. "It came in that."

"Leonardo's of Pisa. Sounds like an Italian restaurant. There's no such place, of course."

"Oh?"

She quick-stepped to her desk, set her fingers to the keyboard, and in a moment was scanning a list of restaurants in Cambridge. "Well, there wouldn't be, would there? It's some kind of stupid joke. Nope, nothing remotely like that name. The address doesn't map, either."

"So why do I feel like I should take it seriously? I'd better bag this, just in case."

While Peller slipped envelope and note into an evidence bag, Montufar returned to his side and gazed at him without expression. "Because you need a vacation. Take some time off, visit your son and his family."

He read the note again through the gloss of the plastic bag. "I don't think so."

"Rick!"

He shot her a surprised look, then laughed. "I didn't mean that. I mean that's not why I'm uneasy. This message. It's a promise."

"That nobody dies?"

"Just the opposite."

Montufar regarded the note again. "I *start* with zero. But after zero . . ."

"Comes one," Peller said. "Nobody dies today, but somebody does die tomorrow, or the day after, or the day after that."

Montufar frowned as she considered the possibility. "Maybe. But it still sounds like a joke to me. Who writes this kind of note?"

Σ

Before long, somebody did die.

That night the snow stopped, the clouds gave way to a clear sky dotted with glittering stars—or at least those bright enough to cut through the light pollution—and on Tuesday morning Marylanders began the slow process of digging out.

Peller wasn't sure if this was a case of March coming in like a lion or of February going out like hyena, laughing at them as it bounded into the distance. Either way, he'd made it home the previous evening courtesy of his F150 four-by-four and experience negotiating the winters of northwest New York. The drive reminded him of a storm from his youth, a snowfall of over a foot and a half followed by two days of sub-zero cold. A freshman in high school, he'd taken on a paper route that year. His father drove him through the predawn chill both days so his customers could get what they'd paid for. Dad had managed a clothing store in town, but he'd grown up on a farm and didn't believe in letting a little thing like spell of bad weather get in the way of work.

Peller began shoveling out in the dim pre-dawn, layered up to keep the cold off until the heat of exertion kicked in. He didn't go in for snow blowers. He disliked the noise and figured the exercise was good for him. Besides, shoveling gave him time to think.

Today he thought about what Montufar had said. His wife Sandra had died four years back in an automobile accident. Her funeral was the last time he had seen Jason, Belinda, and the grandkids. Denver was a long way off. None of them had found the time or money to bridge the space. Or was that just an excuse? Maybe they were all afraid that seeing each other would bring back the pain of their shared loss.

If so, it was a poor excuse.

After two hours of carefully-paced work, he was shoveled out. He rested with a cup of coffee and a cinnamon roll, then ventured back into the cold to start on his neighbor Jerry Souter's walk. Jerry was ninety-three and not quite as handy with a shovel as he used to be. Or at least that's what he said his doctor said, although Jerry himself only took it easy under protest. He had once shown Peller a photograph of himself in a World War II Army uniform. The photographer had captured the defiance in the eyes of the ebony-skinned man, and Peller had thought at the time that if the Allies had had a dozen more men like Jerry, Hitler would still be running. Despite his advanced age, Jerry still stood ramrod-straight, a seasoned veteran whose eyes had seen in a few short years a lifetime of woe. He had insisted from the beginning of their acquaintance that Peller call him Jerry, saying, "Jeremiah makes me sound like a two-hundred-year-old white guy with a beard down to my kneecaps." Eventually Peller became used to the name, but for a long time he had felt as though he were calling one of the Three Kings "Balty".

Peller had just about finished the job when his cell phone went off, a call from dispatch. "Don't tell me," he said. "Another golf clubbing."

"Even better," the dispatcher replied. "A patrolman found a snowplow driver shot in the head on Little Patuxent between the mall and Symphony Woods. We have officers and an ambulance on the scene. The victim's dead."

"Well damn. His plowing wasn't *that* bad, was it? Sorry, shameless joke. As a Marylander, you probably wouldn't get it."

"Wanna bet?"

"I'll be there in about fifteen, twenty minutes," Peller said. As he hurried to his truck, he saw Souter looking out the window. Peller waved, and the old fellow saluted with his coffee cup. Normally Souter would have invited Peller in, but perhaps he could tell from the look on the detective's face that a visit would have to wait.

∑

Symphony Woods was, as its name suggested, a wooded park separating Little Patuxent Parkway and the Merriweather Post Pavilion music theater. On the opposite side of the road stood a series of ten-or-so-story office buildings and beyond them the Columbia Town Center—which Peller had always thought a strange thing to call a shopping mall. Town Center sounded to him like a geographical term, like the point from which mileage was calculated, or the business district on Main Street, around which a town had grown. Whatever it was, thick snow blanketed everything around it except for a thin channel down the middle of the road where the plows had muscled through.

The driver had been shot while plowing the south lanes alongside the park. The vehicle had careened off the road and come to rest blade against an oak trunk.

The snow apparently slowed the truck, because the tree was only lightly scarred. The driver, though, was another matter. He had been shot from the right, the passenger side, and the part of his face not contused from striking the steering wheel was spattered with blood from the exit wound.

The shot must have come from the woods. Scanning the whiteness beneath the trees, Peller noticed a mound about a hundred feet off the side of the road. One of the patrolmen had with some effort slogged through the snow and was now examining the area.

Convenient, Peller thought as he set off down the patrolman's trail, looking for but seeing no sign of disturbance on either side. "Looks kind of like a kid's snow fort," the patrolman remarked as Peller arrived.

Behind the mound—in reality a clumsily-made snow wall—was a hollow of well-stomped snow, a small supply of snowballs, and a path leading out the back. Someone had apparently been as determined to cut through the snow as the officer. The trail led westward towards Broken Land Parkway.

"Get someone to drive around there and see where it comes out," Peller said. "And let's get this area photographed. Maybe the lab can do some digital magic and tell us what size feet were back here."

The officer nodded. "You think the shooter hid back here?"

"Seems likely."

"Pretty fair shot. Not so much the distance, but through the trees at a moving target."

Peller squinted back toward the road. "Doesn't it strike you as a lot of trouble to go through? He wasn't the President. He was a snowplow driver."

"Maybe when we know who he was it'll make some kind of sense."

Not at all sure about that, Peller replied, "Maybe. Let me know what you find at the other end of the trail. I'm going to have another look at the plow."

The wind had picked up. Blowing snow already obscured the trail the officer had broken. Back at the plow, Peller waited for the body to be removed, then took a look around the cab. Very little caught his eye. A pack of chewing gum and a copy of *Fish and Stream* lay on the floor on the passenger's side. The keys were still in the ignition, although the engine had been turned off. Peller made a mental note to ask who had done that. The glove compartment was strangely empty, but he didn't quite know what to expect in the glove compartment of a snowplow.

Peller wondered about the driver's family: who they were, how many they were, what they would do without him. He'd know soon enough, but he always found it disturbing to witness how swiftly a family's world could be demolished.

He wondered what his own family would do if anything happened to him. *Whatever the excuses keeping us apart*, he thought, *not one of them is a good one.*

$$\Sigma$$

When the second letter landed on his desk on Wednesday, March second, Peller almost didn't realize it. Unlike the first, the address was typed, the postmark was Frederick, and the return address claimed the sender was a Mr. F. Leonard. When the latter connected, he called Montufar over. "I think the Italian joint sent us another coupon," he said. Donning a pair of latex gloves, he carefully opened the envelope with a letter opener and pulled out the contents. Again, it was a single sheet of paper, folded neatly into thirds. The contents, like the envelope, were typed:

```
Killed with one shot.
```

"The snowplow driver." Murder being so rare in Howard County, Peller didn't doubt the connection.

Montufar studied the paper as though a novel were written on it. "He's calling attention to the numbers."

Peller rose and walked to the window. As luck would have it, a snowplow was making its way down the road outside. "First zero victims, then one shot. Two comes next. But two what? Could be anything. He's changed what the numbers are attached to. He's changed the location where he mails the notes. He's even changed how he wrote the notes."

"But he didn't change his name. Not exactly, anyway." She joined him at the window, looking upward.

Following her gaze, Peller saw several turkey vultures wheeling overhead. "Leonardo's of Pisa. Mr. F. Leonard. You think he's telling us his name?"

"Not necessarily. That might just be what he wants us to call him."

"It means lion, or something about lions." Before he could pursue the thought, he was called back to his desk by the phone warbling. He snatched up the receiver, said, "Peller," and listened for a moment. "Okay. Corina and I will be over."

Montufar wheeled, ready for action. "What now?"

"I guess the storm is over. There's been another golfing."

Chapter 2

Although not always obvious, there are reasons for our decisions. I, for example, became a mathematician because of my adoptive father. My biological father was killed in the atomic bombing of Nagasaki on August 9, 1945. I was spared only because I was yet in my mother's womb, and on that day she was visiting her parents far outside the city.

After the war, the Americans came to study the results of the radiation, monitoring and testing the survivors over many years. My adoptive father was one of the doctors in that program. He became enamored of my mother, married her, and when he returned to the United States we of course came with him. My love of numbers was born of his influence. And so I became a mathematician and studied arcane aspects of number theory.

Others have come to a similar place through very different causes, and still others have through very similar causes ended up in very different places. Life is not quite so tidy as mathematics.

Then again, many sequences start with the numbers zero and one. Very few continue with two. Perhaps mathematics is less tidy than one might think. Or perhaps life is more so. Σ

The victim, Bess Williams, was a Caucasian female, twenty-eight years old, a good Samaritan dropping off food donations at the Presbyterian church across the street from Centennial Park when she was clobbered from behind. Stunned but not knocked unconscious, she was relieved of her cash, engagement ring, and a gold-chain necklace set with her birthstone, amethyst. After her attacker left, she'd been lucid enough to call 911 on her cell phone.

Having arrived at the crime scene just after Williams was taken to the hospital, Peller and Montufar quickly noticed that there was little to notice. The parking lot had been plowed, although four or five parking places remained half-buried, and a path shoveled to the main door of the church. Half a dozen plastic grocery bags filled with canned goods sat near the door, while three more with contents spilling out lay behind the trunk of Williams's blue Volvo, which was parked parallel to the building near the door. She had apparently been attacked while removing the bags from the trunk. No blood was in evidence; one of the officers at the scene informed the detectives that Williams had been wearing a thick hat.

And she had seen the golf club: a Wilson nine-iron resting on the ground beside her while the attacker, standing over her prone body, rummaged through her purse.

"I'll talk to her," Montufar said. "You should look around some more. Something's odd about this attack."

"As opposed to the previous ones?"

She gave Peller a sidelong glance, lips pinched tight.

He shrugged and shuffled toward the pile of bags by the door. Behind him, he heard Montufar slam the car door and drive off with a squeal of tires.

Peller turned up his collar against the cold. The temperature was in the high twenties and the air still, not bad compared to what he was used to, but he was finding cold weather increasingly unpleasant. *Must be getting old*, he told himself. Although he wasn't sure that at forty-six he was quite ready to think of himself as old.

As the crime scene unit finished work and its members departed, the parking lot grew quiet. The persistent rush of traffic in the distance scarcely registered as he let his eyes play over the area: the church, the bags of food, the car, the winter-bare trees, the snow gently blanketing the yard and piled into Himalayan foothills at the edge of the parking lot.

Montufar was right. Something was odd about the scene, and he knew what it was. "Hey Scott," he called to the photographer who was loading his equipment into the trunk of his car. With a gesture, Peller indicated the entrance to the parking lot. "Did you notice anything over there?"

Squinting into the snow-reflected light, Scott Sahin pondered for a bit, his dark features pulled into a look of concentration. Sahin's parents were from Turkey. He had been born in the U.S., but his given name wasn't Scott. Peller didn't know what it was, only that Scott had grown tired of people butchering it and had settled on "Scott" as something Americans could get right most of the time.

"No, but I see what you mean. There's no sign of anyone entering the parking lot from any other direction, so the attacker must have come in that way."

"And he didn't drive in," Peller said, "or the victim would have heard the car and looked to see who it was."

"Maybe there are some footprints on or near the road."

They headed that direction, scanning the ground as they went. The emergency vehicles had churned the snow into slush, and there was no indication that any walker had passed that way. The road showed only tire ruts.

The road itself was a long lane that led onto the church grounds, lined on one side with tall pines burdened with wet snow and on the other with small trees and bushes half-buried in plowed-up piles. It would have been easy for someone to walk in unobserved. The lane extended beyond the parking lot towards a second building behind the church. Peller walked it and about two hundred feet along found another parking lot entrance flanked by a pair of bare trees. There, as though a car had parked under the leftmost tree, he spotted a set of depressions in the snow. Alongside them he found a single footprint, somewhat smeared.

He motioned to Sahin, who took one look and then returned to retrieve his equipment. As Peller waited, his cell phone went off.

"You got another letter, Rick," a deep, vaguely scratchy voice told him. The voice belonged to Detective Sergeant Eric Dumas, Peller's second-closest associate after Montufar. Montufar and Dumas were his protégés, after a fashion—officially under his command, but in Peller's eyes equal to himself as team members.

"What's the name on the return address?" Peller asked.

"Leon F. Pisano. Another variation on the theme. This one sounds like a lawyer."

"Have you opened it?"

Dumas rattled the paper. "Yep. It says, and I quote, 'A first-born son.' Not very informative."

"And not in keeping with the pattern. We were expecting something about two."

"So he's not just a lunatic, he's a lunatic who can't count."

Peller stared at the lone footprint in the snow, puzzled. "I don't think so. Something else is going on here."

"If you say so. All I know is, it's going to be a challenge protecting all the firstborn sons in the county."

∑

The hospital door closed behind Montufar. She took a deep breath of the cool antiseptic air to calm herself and immediately regretted it. Montufar hated hospitals: the code announcements, the white lab coats and hypocritically-cheerful scrubs, the air itself. All of it reminded her painfully of her mother's long dying. She wondered why she had volunteered to talk to Bess Williams, but she also realized that the woman would probably be more comfortable talking to her than to one of the male detectives. And Peller's keen eye was needed at the crime scene in any case. So she did her best to shut out her surroundings and concentrate on her job.

Mamá would have told me to pray. Mamá would have told me to ask the Blessed Virgin for strength.

Mamá was dead.

Montufar located the bed where Williams was being treated. A nurse just leaving had pulled the curtain around. Montufar nudged it open it far enough to look in.

Her head bandaged, Williams rested in the half-raised bed, nursing a cup of water and gazing blankly at the top of the curtain. Her shoulder-length dark hair spilled haphazardly around her slender face. The sheet was bunched around her waist.

"Bess?"

Williams lowered her eyes to look, but said nothing.

"I'm Corina Montufar. I'm a detective with the Howard County Police. May I come in?" Beckoned by a half-hearted wave of the hand, she stepped in and pulled the curtain shut again. "How are you doing? Are they treating you well?"

"Okay, I guess. It doesn't hurt much anymore."

Montufar pulled a chair over and sat. "We're doing everything we can to find out who did this to you. I know you probably don't feel much like talking, but if it's all right with you I'd like to ask you a few things."

"I didn't see much," Williams said. "He came up behind me. I didn't even know he was there."

"You didn't hear anything?"

She shook her head slowly, took a sip of water. "I guess I was focused on what I was doing."

"You were delivering food donations?"

"Yeah. The church collects for the food bank year round." She laughed, although Montufar thought it sounded forced. "My dad always says no good deed goes unpunished. I guess he's right."

"But you did see something, at least a little bit of something."

"It's a bit fuzzy. I thought something had fallen on me, maybe a tree branch. Maybe the snow broke a branch and it fell on me. I was lying on the ground and then this golf club was there, lying in front of my face. That's when I knew what was happening. I'd heard about the other attacks on the news, you know?"

Montufar nodded.

"He was tugging at my hand. I played dead. That's what you're supposed to do, right? Make them think they got you."

"How long were you there?" Montufar asked.

"I don't know. Maybe five minutes, maybe ten. He didn't rush. He took my necklace and . . ." Williams looked away, choked up. Montufar waited patiently. After another sip of water she continued, "And my engagement ring. I don't know which is worse. My grandmother gave me that necklace." Her eyes drifted back to Montufar. "And my cash, which at least wasn't much, only about fifty dollars, I think."

"Did you know when he was gone?"

She nodded. "He picked up the golf club and walked away. Casually, like he was on the course. He was whistling."

"Did you see him? Can you describe him? Height, weight, clothing?"

"Not really. I was too scared to move, and my head hurt like crazy, but eventually I peeked. He was almost to the road by then, and I don't think I was seeing too clearly. I only remember a sort of grayish blur in the shape of a man. I'd say . . ." Williams put a hand to her forehead as though taking her own temperature. "I don't know. Medium height, I guess. But I could be wrong."

Montufar nodded. "One last thing. I understand you had a pretty good look at the golf club."

"Yeah, that I could see. It was a Wilson nine-iron. But it looked short."

Montufar had no idea if golf clubs came in different lengths. She supposed they must, probably to accommodate players of different heights.

"No, not just short." Williams sounded surprised. "It was actually cut off. I remember now. Like somebody cut it off. It only had about half a handle."

"A sawed-off golf club?" Montufar laughed, then quickly added, "Sorry, it's not funny, I don't suppose."

Williams smiled weakly. "Well. Maybe put that way it is!"

Chapter 3

The word "famous" is seldom used to describe mathematical concepts. There are a few exceptions. Einstein's equation from the Special Theory of Relativity, $E=mc^2$, is rightly regarded as famous. The Golden Ratio might be called famous, although the number of people who have heard of it is far larger than the number who can state its numerical value. Even fewer can state its algebraic expression.

Thus, non-mathematicians are usually hard-pressed to recognize a famous mathematical idea, even when hints are liberally provided.

So it was in this case. Σ

"A sawed-off golf club?" Peller almost laughed. Almost. He held the latest note from Leo, as they had begun to call him, by the corner of the evidence bag. God, but his work had become bizarre of late.

Montufar pulled a chair over to Peller's desk. "He must have cut it off to carry it concealed under his coat."

"I suppose it would look a bit odd, gallivanting around town with a nine-iron in hand. And of course once people started hearing about the attacks, anyone doing so would immediately be bound, gagged, and left on our doorstep."

Eric Dumas sauntered into the conversation, casually flipping a quarter with his right hand. As Peller watched, Dumas gradually increased the height of each toss until he achieved an impressive amplitude of about three feet without a miss. "From what we know so far," Dumas said, "he's something of a magician. Nobody sees him coming, nobody hears him coming. Then bam!" He caught the coin with a swipe of the hand that nearly connected with Montufar's nose.

She glowered at him. "So he walks quietly."

"More than that," Dumas said. "He times his approach just right, when his victim's attention is fixed on something else. Like this." He curled his fingers around the quarter, held up his hand, and blew on it. When he opened his fingers again, the quarter was gone.

Impressed, Montufar looked to his left hand dangling by his side. He brought it up and opened it. Empty. "Where is it?" she asked.

"In your left trouser pocket," Peller said without expression.

Dumas looked like he'd just bitten a lemon. "So much for misdirection."

"It just needs rehearsal. Unfortunately, the mad golfer is little more than a nuisance at the moment." He dropped the letter on the desk and tapped it. "Leo wants to kill somebody. Again."

"Or already has," Montufar added.

Dumas pulled the quarter from his pocket and scowled at it accusingly, as though it had ruined his trick. "No new homicides reported yet," he said. "Wait a minute!"

"Yes," Peller said, deadpan, "it really is the same quarter."

"Exactly. I mean, it could be. What if Leo *is* the mad golfer?"

Montufar looked at him as if he'd lost his mind.

"No, seriously," Dumas continued. "How likely is it we'd have two nutcases running around at the same time?"

"It happens," Peller said. "There isn't anything to connect the two cases aside from their weirdness."

"And the thought that's gone into the crimes."

"True, but the golfer is after money," Montufar objected. "Leo looks like a serial killer."

Peller looked away. "Don't even think that," he said. But that spectre had already taken up residence in his own mind, and silence wouldn't banish it. Most murders were ghosts of yesterday merely awaiting exorcism. Serial killings were ghosts lurking in the shadows of tomorrow, intent on transforming morning into darkest night.

Montufar said nothing. Dumas studied his quarter in silence for few moments, then half-heartedly repeated the disappearing quarter trick. In spite of the gloom that had settled over them, this time he pocketed the coin flawlessly. "Misdirection," he said, continuing his previous line of thought. "He gives us something to think about other than what he's really up to."

"We're getting ahead of ourselves," Peller said. "We don't have many facts in either case. But point taken, Eric. It could be one person behind both crime sprees. Something to keep in mind, perhaps."

Dumas finished the thought for him. "But not to run with just yet. Agreed." He tried the coin trick one last time.

And the quarter fell to the floor with the unconvincing clatter of base metal.

Σ

Montufar drew the task of visiting Maggie Patterson, widow of Mark Patterson, mother of Mandy and Mark Junior. Montufar wondered why people would inflict identical initials upon their children. At least they weren't like some she'd encountered in her law enforcement career, truly bizarre appellations bestowed by aging hippies or drug addicts.

She recruited one of her junior underlings, Detective Theresa Swan, to accompany her, and the pair arrived at the Patterson home just after three o'clock. As Montufar rang the doorbell of the white and sky-blue bungalow surrounded by incongruously large maples and oaks, Detective Swan shifted nervously. "I've never done a murder investigation before," she said quietly.

"Don't worry," Montufar reassured her. "I'll ask the questions. Well, most of them. Chime in if you think I'm overlooking something, but otherwise focus on observing and taking notes."

When Patterson opened the door, she proved to be a tall, lanky blonde with a corpse-like face: thin, bony, creased, and expressionless. Montufar guessed this wasn't her normal look but one she'd be wearing for some time to come. Her husband, after all, had been shot to death on the job. And all he did was drive a snowplow.

Of all the stupid ways to die, Montufar thought. She introduced herself and Swan and asked if they might come in. Patterson motioned them in with a slight nod. Inside, Montufar found the living room to be small and simple, but comfortable enough. The furniture was old and a bit worn but clean, upholstered in red and yellow floral patterns. A grandfather clock that appeared to be a genuine heirloom ticked off seconds at one end of the room; a modest TV quietly occupied the other. The detectives and their host sat on opposite sides of a mission-style coffee table whose cherry finish suggested it was newer than the rest of the furnishings.

"I know it sounds like a platitude," Montufar began, "but we want you to know how very sorry we are for your loss. We're doing everything we can to find out who killed your husband and bring him to justice."

Patterson cupped her chin in her hands. "I know you are. I have a cousin with the police down in Richmond. Anything I can do to help, just let me know."

"I guess the first thing is if you know of anyone who might have wanted Mark dead."

"No. Oh, there were people who didn't like him very much. He was opinionated and not always polite. But I can't see anyone hating him that much."

"Opinionated how?"

"Every way." She actually chuckled and her face lit up for a moment, but the light slipped away as quickly as it had come. "He thought most everyone was a moron in some way or another. He didn't much like politicians, lawyers, doctors. Police." She said the last a bit hesitantly, then continued, "Priests, ministers, and rabbis. He thought our minister was a dunce. He only went to church because of me, I think."

"What church do you attend?"

"Columbia Presbyterian. It's a bit of a drive, but it was the church I went to when I was little."

Montufar and Swan exchanged glances. Was this coincidence or something more? Maybe Dumas was onto something after all.

"What is it?" Patterson asked.

"Probably nothing. It's just there was an incident at that church earlier today. I expect you'll hear about it before too long."

Patterson didn't seem too interested. She gazed out the window at the melting snow, not really looking, perhaps only waiting for something, something that would never again happen.

"Who would have known Mark would have been plowing that area?" Montufar asked. "And how far in advance would they have known it?"

"I'm not sure. I never asked him much about that job, and he didn't talk about it much. He only did it to make some extra money over the winter. He was really a carpenter, but work is always slow this time of year, and with the economy as bad as it's been, even the busy seasons haven't been too busy. Probably only the people he works with would have known."

"Was there a routine?"

"Not really," Patterson replied. "He'd get a call when they wanted him to report in. You'd know the call was coming if you paid attention to the weather reports.

He got the call about four in the afternoon the day before he was killed. The snow started later that evening. I guess he would have been out there all night, but I couldn't tell you where he worked or when he took breaks or anything like that."

She leaned back into the sofa and exhaled heavily. "I don't think anyone wanted him dead," she said. It came out more forcefully than anything else she had said, which wasn't saying much but suggested that she really wanted to believe it.

Montufar pondered this for a moment, perhaps for too long, because Swan quietly asked the obvious question: "Then why was he shot?"

Patterson shrugged. "Because he was there. Wrong place, wrong time. It's a busy road. It could have been anyone."

"Not just then," Swan replied. "Very few people were out and about."

Patterson slowly shifted her gaze to Swan, to Montufar, back to Swan.

"Except for the plows," she said.

Σ

The firstborn son turned out to be Andrew Carrington, a twenty-six-year-old HVAC technician in line to take over the family business a decade or two in the future when his father James retired. The young man had been shot at close range in a back corridor at the Columbia Mall early on Thursday, March third while on his way out from completing a job fixing a balky thermostat. He had been on-site before the mall opened for his first job of the day, and, as it had turned out, his last. There had been no witnesses to the shooting, although several mall employees had heard the shot and mall security had arrived on the scene within minutes.

Peller scrutinized the area closely but found nothing to suggest anything beyond the bare fact that a young man had died violently. Aside from the body sprawled on the floor in a pool of blood, the corridor was so nondescript that it might as well not have been there. Carrington could have been lying in an undifferentiated expanse of gray suffused with mist.

Peller let his eyes play over every inch of the body: the head twisted sideways as though still looking for the assailant, the left arm outstretched as though to break the fall, the right leg pulled up with the foot turned inward, probably in a last-ditch effort to recover balance. The shot had come from behind and penetrated the skull almost dead center. Peller was sure he'd never known what happened.

A sudden cacophony of voices jarred Peller from his thoughts. Turning, he saw a man built like a linebacker trying to push his way through a wall of police officers who were struggling to hold him back. "You can't come in here, sir!" one of the officers said while another yelled, "Stay back! Stay back!"

"Let me through!" he barked. "What's going on? Who's that on the floor? Damn it, let me through!"

He forced the officers a few feet forward, then stopped and stared in horror at the body. "Oh my God," he whispered, then cried, "Andrew! Andrew!" He tried to take another step, but the officers had rearranged themselves to better restrain him, and he couldn't move. Peller stepped between the man and Andrew's body. The newcomer was a good four inches taller than he, forcing him to look up. "Who are you?" he asked, keeping his voice low.

"My son. What the hell happened? That's my son!"

Peller looked back at the dead man. "Mr. Carrington, we should go somewhere else to discuss this."

Carrington drew back a fist, but the officers yanked him backwards before he could land the punch. "I'm not leaving my son!" he bellowed. "Who did this? Tell me who did this. I'll kill him!"

"This is a crime scene," Peller said sharply. "You can't be here. Let's go to the security office. We can talk there."

Carrington glared at Peller, who met him with a face of stone. Finally the father slumped. "Okay," he said. The officers relaxed their grips on him. He turned away, then with a massive thrust he threw them off. "Where's security?"

The mall security guard who had been assigned to the crime scene led Peller and Carrington through a maze of service corridors to the mall office, then through the public area to a private office.

"This is Janet's office, but she won't be in for a couple of hours," the guard said as he opened the door. "That give you enough time?"

Peller nodded, and the man exited. The room was nothing more than a large cubicle with barely enough room for a desk and a couple of chairs, but its regular occupant had made an attempt to cheer it with a potted African violet under a tiny grow light and a framed set of prints of Monet's bridge in various seasons. Peller doubted that they would help today.

"Won't you sit down, Mr. Carrington?" he asked. "Can I get you some water?"

Carrington slumped into a chair and fixed his eyes on the floor. "No thanks."

"What brought you here?" Peller asked.

Carrington worked his jaw for a moment, as though about to spit out something inedible. "Andrew should have been on to his next job. The dispatcher couldn't raise him. I thought maybe something had gone wrong with the job, so I was coming out to help." He looked up suddenly. "Do you know who did this?" he demanded.

Peller shook his head. "It's too early. There weren't any witnesses. Tell me about your son."

"He was a good kid. There's no reason for this to happen. Nobody would have wanted to hurt him." Tears slipped from Carrington's eyes. He angrily wiped them away.

"So I guess he was never in any serious trouble?"

"No, never. He was the quiet one. Smart, good with numbers. His younger brother was the one who got into scraps, not him."

Peller felt a chill run down his back. "Andrew was your oldest?"

"No, his sister Maria is the oldest. He was our second."

"Firstborn son, though." Anger boiling up from his gut, Peller turned away to prevent Carrington seeing.

"Yeah," Carrington said, tears filling his eyes. "Firstborn son."

Σ

When finally Peller dragged himself back to headquarters and up to his desk, he found Montufar waiting for him, a new bagged letter in her hands.

"Damn him," Peller said, knowing what it was before looking. "Damn him, damn him, damn him! What's the number now? Seventeen?"

"Two." Montufar read it: "'Two shots, two kills. Slower students may wish to ponder my namesake.'"

"Namesake? What the hell does *that* mean?"

"The envelope was printed on—are you ready for this?—an old dot matrix printer. So was the letter. The return address is a nonexistent street in Bel Air. The name he gives this time is Leonidas Pissaro."

Peller rubbed his eyes. "And that's supposed to mean something to us?"

"I think so. I just got my hands on this a few minutes ago, so I haven't had time to research it. But I'm betting the name will tell us something important."

"All right, look into it. I have to . . ."

Before he could finish, a quiet female voice behind him interrupted. "I need to see both of you in my office right away."

The voice belonged to Captain Whitney Morris, head of the Criminal Investigations Division, and in spite of her subdued tone Peller knew the matter was serious. Not a difficult deduction under the circumstances, but it was more than that. There was a tension in the captain's face that he had only seen on the worst of days.

"Right away," he agreed, turning to follow her. Montufar fell into line behind. Morris led them into her office in the corner of the building. It had windows on two sides, an ample desk, bookcases crammed with heavy volumes on law and police procedure and management practices, and four chairs for visitors. Her desk was the cleanest one in the place, with little more on it than her computer, a notepad, and photos of her husband and three children.

The last one in, Montufar closed the door behind her and they all sat. Morris took a moment to regard the photos, then said, "Over the past five years, Howard County has averaged three point eight murders per year. This Leo guy is going to shatter that statistic in just a few days if we don't stop him. Between him and the golf attacks, we're getting some dirty looks from the powers-that-be. And the press appears to be gearing up for a feeding frenzy."

She paused a moment to let it sink in. As if it had to, Peller thought. "Tell me what you need to resolve these cases."

He glanced at Montufar. She shrugged, almost imperceptibly. "Mostly time," he replied.

"Which is the one luxury we don't have," the captain said.

"Everything has to be priority one. Ballistics, M.E., the works. The notes haven't told us anything helpful yet, but Corina is researching the names he's been using. The latest note suggests that's important. Unfortunately, the only other constants are the numbers."

Morris picked up her pen and clicked it a few times. "I can reassign the golfer case."

"It might be connected," Montufar told her.

"How?"

Peller shook his head. "We don't know that. It's just an off-the-cuff idea Eric had. He thought it odd that two nutcases would be committing high-profile crimes at the same time."

After a few more clicks of the pen, which Peller found vaguely irritating, Morris made her decision. "Rick, you work the murders full-time. Eric can ride point on the golfer muggings. Corina, I want you to switch-hit. That way if there is a connection, we won't miss it. I'll reassign anything else the three of you have on your plates. If you need any additional support, I'll get it for you."

She waited for the detectives to rise from their chairs, then asked, "What's the number on this latest note?"

"Two," Peller told her.

"Two what?"

"Two shots, two kills."

She slumped in her chair. A bad sign, Peller thought. Captain Morris wasn't generally one to show even a hint of weakness.

Chapter 4

What is a number? This question is not one most people ask. Number is such an integral part of our intellectual backdrop that the concept scarcely needs explaining. Yet if you had to define number, how would you do it?

Most likely, you would start by referring to how many items are in a group: four chairs, ten people, a thousand stars shining in the sky. You would intuitively grasp a key mathematical concept: number is a generic property of sets.

But when someone says, "Eight," you would still want to know, "Eight what?" whereas I would not. Eight of this or eight of that are both eight, which is sufficient.

Or it was, before it came down to eight human lives. Σ

Dumas had given up on quarters and began working with half-dollars. Easier to grip, he told Montufar, but not as easy to palm. He tried a vanish for her and got her approval, which was gratifying but merely a start. Peller was the tough one to fool. His eye was far too keen, spookily so sometimes, Dumas thought, good for detective work but rotten if you happened to be an amateur magician—and not a very skilled one, he had to admit—with Peller in your audience.

"So anyway," Dumas said once the trick was over, "I think we should ask for extra patrols in the area around Centennial Park. The mad golfer doesn't seem to stray too far from the park. What we really need are cops poking their noses into secluded corners. If we can make life more difficult for him, he might make a mistake."

Montufar concurred, but something else was on her mind. "Why Centennial Park, do you think?"

"Convenience? Maybe he lives in the area."

She gazed upward, a faraway look on her face. Dumas watched her with admiration. He had taken some ribbing from other men in the department over the way he looked at her when she wasn't aware of it, but it wasn't physical attraction that drew his gaze. Well, not mere physical attraction, anyway. He did find her easy on the eyes. But it was more admiration for how her mind worked, the knack she had for drawing together the seemingly disparate pieces of a puzzle and almost magically making sense out of them. That was it, he thought: she was a better magician than he, only she worked magic inside her head instead of with physical objects.

"The Fairway Hills golf course is right there, too," she said. "Maybe that gives him some cover, makes him seem less suspicious. But then, why would he need cover? He carries a concealed sawed-off golf club, not a golf bag. Let's look at a map."

Dumas turned to his computer and in a moment had the requested map displayed. The park proper was nearly a mile wide east to west and half a mile wide north to south, although a part of it extended nearly a mile north. The centerpiece of the park, Centennial Lake, stretched from east to west most of the way. Residential areas abutted the park north, east, and south, while the golf course connected to the park on the southeast corner. The golf course and additional parklands extended another mile to the south, weaving around additional neighborhoods.

"That park would give him access to a huge area," Dumas said, tracing it with his finger not quite touching the monitor.

"A lot to patrol," Montufar added.

"A number of these areas are on the high side of middle class, too. We could put some plainclothes officers out there, make them look like they have something worth stealing."

"How do we provide backup? The bait would be working without a net."

"That's one wild mixed metaphor," Dumas laughed. He pushed his chair back from his desk and stood. "I guess we'd better ponder that, though. Meanwhile, I'm going to go through the incidents to date one more time, see if I can find any patterns. I don't think we'll catch this nutcase unless we do it red-handed. Redclubbed, actually." He grinned, then abruptly stopped when he realized Montufar wasn't.

"Good thing your magic tricks are better than your jokes," she said.

Σ

When the ballistics and medical reports arrived in Peller's inbox on the morning of Friday, March fourth, they confirmed the pattern so far followed by Leo: that of avoiding any pattern whatsoever. Mark Patterson, the snowplow driver, had apparently been killed by a shot from a distance fired from a military-style M40 sniper rifle, while Andrew Carrington, the firstborn son, had been shot at fairly close range with a thirty-eight. Even stranger, although so far Patterson appeared to be a victim of opportunity, Andrew Carrington had clearly been lured to his death. The thermostat he was going to fix proved to have been sabotaged; the store in which it was installed was one he regularly served.

The utter lack of consistency infuriated Peller. It was plain to him that Leo was toying with him and enjoying the game immensely. If it weren't for the two bodies lying cold and still in the morgue, it might have been taken for an elaborate practical joke, with Leo laughing at his frustration.

Then again, that same lack of consistency highlighted the one consistent aspect of the case: the name. And there, Montufar had quickly scored an easy victory. So easy, in fact, that it, too, was irritating. Extra credit points. He could almost hear Leo chuckling.

Σ

Immediately after the meeting with Captain Morris, Montufar had performed a single internet search, printed out the results, and brought them to Peller, who scarcely had time to reach his own desk ahead of her.

"Look at this," she said, slapping the pages down. "Leonardo's of Pisa, Mr. F. Leonard, Leon F. Pisano, and Leonidas Pissaro are *all* based on this guy. Leonardo Pisano Bigollo. Also known as Leonardo of Pisa, also known as Fibonacci. A mathematician, born in 1170, died in 1250. So obviously *he's* not our man. But look at this." She pointed to a paragraph a third of the way down the page. "Fibonacci series," Peller read. "Never heard of it. Okay, let's see: it starts with zero, followed by one, and each number thereafter is the sum of the previous two. Zero, one, one, two, three, five, eight, thirteen, twenty-one, thirty-four, fifty- . . . my God."

"That's where the numbers come from."

Peller looked up at her. She looked quite pleased, and so she should be, he thought, except for one thing. "Good work, Corina. Now if we just knew what the numbers mean."

"I know. But there's a pattern in the numbers, and he told us what it was. This series. That's one key to his plan. Is there a second key as well, a pattern in what the numbers mean? Is he telling us that through these notes as well?"

The idea was definitely worth considering. "Okay, let's think about this. The first day was zero, so—zero victims. Next day was the snowplow driver—one shot. Then the firstborn son, two victims and two shots." Peller pushed himself back from the desk, rather more forcefully than necessary. "Two and two. Why isn't that four? If three, five, and eight come next, will it be three victims, five shots, and an eighth-born son?"

Montufar perched on the edge of his desk, her eyes staring off at nothing. "Or five sisters, with eight cups of poisoned tea, at three in the afternoon? Five cars with eight passengers in three parking lots? It doesn't have to be simple. It probably won't be. He could work those numbers in all kinds of ways. For a long, long time."

Peller gazed at her until she met his eyes. For the first time since he had met her, she was utterly still. In the silence, he knew they were both thinking the same thing: this was very, very bad. By giving them the sequence—an infinite sequence—had Leo shown them that he planned to go on killing without limit.

Σ

What he really needed to know was why Mark Patterson and Andrew Carrington were chosen for death. Did they have some connection to Leo? It seemed unlikely. At least, no connections between the victims had so far surfaced. Maggie Patterson had suggested to Montufar that her husband had died simply because he was a target of convenience. That was possible. But could Carrington, a firstborn son, simply have been a target of convenience? No. Leo knew his next victim when he wrote the note because he knew how the number figured into the killing.

Which could point to another inconsistency: one victim a target of opportunity, one planned in advance.Peller fished a bottle of aspirin out of his desk drawer. He was going to need it. Before he could get the bottle open, the call he'd been dreading came in.

Two shots. Two victims.

$$\Sigma$$

The line separating Howard County from Baltimore County is in fact the Patapsco River. At the end of its course, the Patapsco flares into the estuary of the Chesapeake Bay where Baltimore's Inner Harbor lies in the heart of the city. Eight or so miles upstream from the harbor, a railroad crosses the river at Ilchester Road, and about a quarter mile further upstream, the river rushes noisily over a spillway. It is secluded, well-forested, perhaps a good spot to get away from the pressures of work during lunch break. Today, at least three people had visited: a retired man who lived a couple miles north of the river who had been walking for exercise, and the dead couple he happened upon.

Peller parked at the rail bridge where a smallish parking lot lay on the north side of the road. Several other vehicles were already there: a couple of police cruisers, a crime scene unit van, and a Lincoln Zephyr. He walked along the tracks to the crime scene, which was engulfed in a rush of activity that somehow seemed an extension of the spillway. The weather had warmed considerably since the snowstorm and most of the snow had already melted, swelling the river perceptibly but not to flood stage. The ground fairly squished beneath his feet. A few birds twittered somewhere overhead.

The victims were a male and a female: he solidly built, of fair complexion but with a dark mop of hair; she short and Mediterranean. They were sprawled haphazardly on the bank of the river, close together, face up, each killed by a single shot to the forehead. The ground in the area was a confusion of smeared mud and trampled undergrowth. Crime scene tape cordoned off a few areas where individual footprints were in evidence.

"Do we know who they are?" Peller asked one of the officers, a young black woman who looked almost lost in her uniform.

"The man's name is Zachary Rymer and the woman's is Helen Kamber. They both had driver's licenses on them." She directed a hesitant look towards the bodies before turning her attention to the river.

"First murder scene?" Peller asked.

The officer nodded.

"Detective Rick Peller," he said, tapping himself on the chest. "What's your name?"

"Sheila Crane," she said. "Rookie." Then, with a nervous laugh, she added, "Very."

"Well, Sheila, I'll tell you the secret. Don't think too hard about it and you'll do okay."

She nodded her thanks.

Returning his attention to the victims, Peller took in their manner of dress. Rymer wore a pale blue button-down shirt, khaki slacks, black dress shoes, and a North Face jacket over the top. Kamber was clothed in a green knee-length skirt and a pale printed blouse—leaves?— but it was so splattered with mud that the pattern was almost hidden. The mud was odd. It looked as though it had been thrown at her or kicked onto her after she fell, whereas Rymer's clothes were almost pristine.

Leaving Crane's side, he examined the ground farther out from the bodies. Police personnel had entered the scene via the railroad, which allowed them easy access and prevented them from disturbing the area before it had been photographed and examined. The victims would have walked in the same way, he figured. They weren't dressed for scrambling through the woods or along the riverbank. The Lincoln was probably theirs.

As for Leo—Peller had no doubt this was his handiwork, since it fit the note so well—he would also have come back this way. But how would he have known he would find the requisite two victims here?

Clearly this wasn't the first time the couple had come here, and Leo knew it. Somehow.

Peller found Crane bagging up something. "What's that?" he asked.

"A ring. We found it just over here," she indicated a spot about ten feet from

Kamber's body. "It looks like costume jewelry to me."

Peller squinted at it. "Maybe. What do you think? The killer takes it off of her finger, decides it's not real, and drops it?"

"Probably. It has to be hers. If it had been lost out here for any length of time, I don't think it would look this good."

Interesting, he thought. Leo was a killer, not a thief. Unless Dumas was right and Leo was also the mad golfer. "Have it checked out as soon as possible. Could be important. Also, we need to go over that Lincoln Zephyr back at the parking lot. It could have belonged to one of these two. Can you pass all that along for me?"

"Will do. But what are you going to do?"

Peller gazed thoughtfully at the river, then did an about-face. "I'm going for a walk," he replied, starting toward the tracks.

Σ

By all rights, Montufar should have accompanied Peller to the murder scene, except that twenty minutes before he got his call, Dumas got a call of his own: another golfing had been reported, this time in the back yard of a house on the northern edge of Centennial Park. "You'd better come with me on this one," he told Montufar. "The victim is a woman. She's apparently in hysterics."

So they hurried to the Lakeside Court residence, a good-sized two-story home near the end of the street, nestled among a collection of trees and bordered in the rear by what looked like a forest but in fact was simply a stand of trees that ran along the edge of the park.

They parked in the driveway behind the police cruiser that had arrived on the scene earlier. A male officer ws standing guard at the door and let them in. Dumas motioned Montufar to go first, figuring it would be better if she did most of the talking.

Inside, they passed beneath cathedral ceilings to the living room, which was populated by a collection of wood furnishings tastefully upholstered in creamy white fabric. Deep rugs dotted an expanse of glossy oaken parquetry. Dumas guessed all of it was beyond a detective's means. Not that it suited his tastes anyway.

A tall, angular woman with the build of a personal trainer, and a clothing ensemble to match, was muttering to herself as she circled the room. She seemed to take no notice of the newcomers. Her relentless activity reminded Dumas of a tiger pacing about its cage. He wondered if she was going to stop anytime soon.

A female officer standing to one side of the room stared at the floor as though deliverance might perhaps come from that direction. Dumas motioned Montufar forward, then took up a position next to the officer. He mouthed, "How long?", surreptitiously indicating the victim. The woman raised her eyebrows and rolled her eyes expressively.

"Hi," Montufar said, approaching the woman. "I'm Corina Montufar from the Howard County Police. You've had some trouble here."

The woman didn't stop moving. Rapidly, she said, "Thanks, thanks for coming. I'm Regina. Regina Collins. You know I was robbed? Right here in my own house! My husband's in California on a business trip and I'm here all by myself and I've been *robbed!*"

Montufar gave Dumas a confused look. He shrugged. All the dispatcher had said was there had been another golf club attack at this location. It sure didn't look as though the woman had been clubbed.

"We're going to help you," Montufar told Collins. "Why don't we sit down and you can tell me what happened."

Collins continued her frantic back-and-forth. "No, that's okay. You sit, I'd rather not. I'll tell you what happened. I was *robbed!*"

Montufar sat down gingerly on the edge of the sofa—almost, Dumas thought, as though not to wrinkle the upholstery. "What were you doing just before you were robbed?"

"I was out back, of course. I had to get the cat back in the house. He belongs to my husband. I wanted him to give him away when we got married, but no, he wouldn't do it. He sheds on everything. And he's black. That cat hates me. Dumb animal always manages to escape. I bent over to grab him, and when I stood up there he was."

"The cat?" Dumas asked, having lost count of the male pronouns.

"The burglar! He was standing right next to me. Leering at me. Scared me to death!"

"Now wait a minute," Dumas said before Montufar could react. "You say he was leering at you?" He exchanged glances with Montufar, who shook her head. This didn't sound like the mad golfer at all.

"Well, I was just in my underwear. So I guess that's why he was looking. But what was he doing there in the first place? Him and that golf club?"

Dumas didn't want to ask.

Montufar apparently did. "Wait. You went outside in your underwear?"

Collins stopped and gave Montufar a curious look, as though she couldn't decide whether to be surprised by the question or astounded at the questioner's stupidity. "What? You never wear a bikini?"

"Never mind. Tell me about the golf club."

"It was a golf club. I don't play golf. It was just this golf club. He was holding it up like he was going to hit me with it. When I stood up and saw him, he didn't move. Just stood there staring at my boobs." She paused and cast a sideways glance at Dumas. He quickly turned to look at the fireplace that monopolized one wall of the room. "Then he put the club down and said, "If you give me your cash and jewelry, I won't hurt you. Or your cat.'"

"Your husband's cat," Dumas said, deadpan.

"Cat, yes. He threatened the cat. Of all things. Like I would have cared. Well, maybe I would have. I'd have a hard time explaining to Josh what happened to his cat. So I did what he said. He followed me into the house—right to my bedroom, which believe me was the last place I wanted to go with him right there behind me! But that's where the money and jewelry were. Once he had them, he left. By the front door, if you can believe that."

"What time was this?" Montufar asked.

"I don't know. Maybe nine o'clock? What time is it now?" She looked around for a clock, but there was nothing so mundane in the living room.

The woman officer glanced at her watch. "Ten-fifteen," she volunteered, then immediately looked sorry that she'd consented to be part of the conversation.

Montufar patted the seat next to her, inviting Collins to sit, which she finally if grudgingly did. "I guess you got a pretty good look at him, then?"

"Yes. But I can't remember much now. I was so upset."

"Try anyway. Whatever you remember might help us catch him."

"Well." Collins looked up at the ceiling, eyes narrowed. "He wasn't as tall as me. I'm six-one, so I'd guess he was maybe five-ten or five-eleven. Looked like he was in good shape, not overweight anyway. Dark brown hair. Clean-shaven. Hazel eyes.

Maybe thirty years old, maybe a bit older." Unexpectedly, she grinned at Montufar. "He was dressed like he was actually playing golf. Kind of old-fashioned. And an overcoat, unbuttoned. Made me think of Cary Grant in *Bringing up Baby*. Have you ever seen that movie? Hysterical!"

If Montufar was rattled by the machine-gun speech, she didn't show it. "Can't say I have. What about the golf club?"

The mention of the club seemed to disturb Collins. She leapt to her feet and began pacing again. "I told you. I don't golf."

"Let me help you. Iron or wood?"

"Oh. Iron, I guess. It was metal, and skinny."

"What about the handle?"

Collins stopped and gave Montufar another one of her looks. "The *handle*? I don't know, it was a handle. That wasn't what he was going to hit me with."

"How long was it?"

Collins pulled her hair out of its ponytail and redid it. "I don't know. Really, I wasn't looking at the handle."

"That's all right," Montufar assured her. "You've already given us a lot of information. We're going to want you to sit down with a sketch artist. If we can get a decent picture of this guy, we'll have a much better chance of finding him."

Once they were outside, Dumas walked to the end of the driveway and took a look up and down the street. "We'll have to canvass the neighborhood, see if anyone saw him. But nobody did, I'm pretty sure. He came in from the park and probably after he was out the door he circled around and went back into the park."

Montufar likewise gazed about. "Agreed. Although it looks pretty quiet. He might have risked parking down the street."

Deadpan, Dumas suggested, "Maybe we should reconstruct the crime. Cat and all."

"Why?" Montufar asked with a grin. "The fluorescent yellow sports bra wasn't good enough? You want to see her in her real underwear?"

He glanced back at the house. "No," he replied. "Not particularly."

Σ

What bothered Peller about the murders by the river, and what set him off upstream along the railroad tracks, was the lack of access to the area. Bordered by the river to the east and heavily forested, the only obvious way in was from the small parking lot under the rail bridge at Ilchester Road. But if the killer had parked there, his victims might have known they weren't the only ones about. The murder of Mark Patterson, the snowplow driver, suggested that Leo preferred stealth. Even if the couple had been shot at close range, Leo would have wanted to catch them by surprise.

He wondered, therefore, if there were some way into the area from the north, and following the tracks for about half a mile gave him the answer: sort of. It looked like at least a few people had come this way over time. Beneath the oak, maple, and ash—all barren of leaves at this time of year—he noticed the occasional discarded candy wrapper, aluminum can, or dilapidated sheet of newsprint. Then, half a mile from the crime scene, he noticed a large house partially hidden by the woods a football field or more to the west.

The vaguest hint of a trail seemed to stretch from where he was towards the house, but it may have been nothing, or possibly a game trail. A few sharp cracks caught his attention; then he spotted the doe picking her way through the woods.

It was at least worth a look, so he pushed his way along the might-be-a-trail, brushing branches out of his way and getting snagged a couple of times on blackberry thorns hidden in the understory. The house, when he came to it, was a three-story brick monstrosity with a four-car garage and its own parking lot. Someone, Peller mused, must have money here. He took his time circling to the other side of the house, looking over the grounds. The lawn and soil underneath were damp, and in shaded areas patches of snow remained. A four-foot pile of dirty snow marked the end of the parking lot farthest from the house.

Of greater interest was the private drive meandering into the woods to the west. Through the trees, Peller glimpsed several other big houses. Somewhere that drive would connect to a road. He would have to check a map, but clearly there was a way to get to the crime scene from the north, if one didn't mind walking for a mile or two.

"Who are you?"

Peller nearly jumped at the sharp voice behind him. When he turned, he was confronted by a woman dressed in a powder blue warm-up suit who was pointing a handgun at his forehead. He put his hands up. People expected that when they trained a gun on someone. "Rick Peller," he said matter-of-factly, "Howard County police."

She gave him a skeptical once-over. "Where's your uniform?"

"I'm a detective. I don't wear a uniform."

"Got ID?"

"If you'll let me get it."

She nodded but didn't lower the gun. He hoped she knew what she was doing with it as he got out his shield and showed it to her. Warily, she lowered the gun. "What are you doing here?"

"There was an incident back in the woods along the track," he said. "Did you happen to see anyone walk through here earlier today?"

She shook her head. "Only person I've seen walking through here is you. What kind of incident?"

"A couple was murdered. It's possible the killer came into the area through here."

The woman put her hand to her throat as a sickly look crossed her face. "Oh my God."

"Don't worry," Peller told her, "there's reason to think he was specifically after these victims. It's not likely he'll be back. We'll be sending someone around to talk with you and your neighbors later." He eyed the gun for a moment, then said, "I have to be going."

The woman nodded absently, and he left her standing there, pointing the gun at the ground.

Chapter 5

Mathematicians deal with infinities all the time. But that's the abstract world of mathematics. Whether infinities exist in nature is a philosophical issue, one that has been debated for centuries without resolution.

In the world of human life, the subject is not an issue. We do not live forever. We do not have infinite powers. Even the sun which gives us life and the Earth which sustains that life are finite creatures.

So even a series of crimes based upon an infinite sequence must sooner or later end. Σ

Nobody got much of a weekend. Captain Morris pulled the strings required to get a lot of things done over the following twenty-four hours, and on Saturday she joined the three detectives to review the results.

The weapon in the most recent murder was identified as a nine-millimeter handgun, probably fired from a distance of around fifty feet. The victims—Zachary Rymer and Helen Kamber—had, according to one of Kamber's co-workers, been seeing each other for a few months. Rymer had been an accountant with a small firm in Ellicott City; Kamber, an assistant manager at a deli down the street, where the two had met. On Kamber's days off she would meet him and sometimes the two would wander off for a while, although never long enough for Rymer to be late returning to the office.

Until the day they were killed.

The ring was identified by a relative as a gift to Kamber from Rymer. It was nothing fancy, just an agate set in a low-carat gold band, but she had treasured it.

Very little new turned up with regard to the robbery. Detectives had knocked on every door in the neighborhood only to learn that no one was home, outside, or looking out the window during the critical time period, so nobody had seen anything of use. A list of stolen jewelry had been drawn up and was being distributed to law enforcement agencies and pawnshops. A sketch had been completed which, Regina Collins remarked, "Was so good it was scary."

"I think," Montufar suggested after the evidence had been reviewed, "that we might be ahead to release the sketch, and mention that the murders are based on the Fibonacci sequence."

Morris shook her head. "Sketch, yes. But we don't want to inspire crackpots, homicidal or otherwise."

"I agree," Peller said. "If we do that we're likely to get a million notes. Remember Jack the Ripper. We'll have no idea which ones are real—if any of them are."

"We will if we withhold any other information," Montufar pointed out. "We don't have to say what the numbers refer to. We don't even have to say that we've been receiving notes. We just say that these murders appear to have a connection to the Fibonacci series."

"Which accomplishes?" Morris asked.

Before Montufar could reply, Dumas rode to her rescue. "It tells Leo that we've figured it out. He wanted us to figure it out. He told us that in the last note. So now that we have, we have to let him know."

Morris pondered this. "Which may change the game somehow, but that's his call. We can't predict how it changes the game. I just don't know." She looked to Peller, eyebrows raised.

He spread his hands and shrugged.

"Two possibilities," Montufar continued. "One, he thinks he's smarter than we are. Once he knows we figured out the numbers, he'll get mad. That makes it more likely he'll make a mistake. Two, as Eric said, he wants us to figure it out. We did, so he moves to the next thing we're supposed to figure out. That gives us more information and moves us closer to apprehending him."

"You think he wants to be caught?" Morris asked.

"Not necessarily. He could be playing chicken with us. But either way, the result is the same. The more information we get him to give us, the closer we get to him."

Dumas was nodding in agreement with Montufar, and although Peller was noncommittal Morris knew he trusted Montufar's instincts. "Okay," she told them. "We'll call a press conference for this afternoon, and put both the sketch and the number thing out there."

Σ

Following the press conference there was little else to do, and since he was effectively on call 24-7 until Leo was caught, Peller told Morris he was going to go home and get some rest before anything else happened.

"Just keep your cell phone charged," she told him.

He stopped at a deli for a crab cake sandwich, a bag of chips, and a soda, which he ate sitting in his car in the parking lot before driving home. When he arrived, he saw Jerry Souter next door in his favorite rocker, one of three stationed on the old man's front porch. Peller waved to Souter, and Souter motioned him over.

As Peller climbed the steps to the porch, Souter asked, "Want some iced tea?"

"A bit cool for that, isn't it?"

"Nah. It got all the way to sixty-three today. Almost summer."

Peller laughed. "You talk like you didn't grow up around here."

"I growed up lots of places," Souter replied with a wink. "You look like death warmed over. Sit awhile."

Peller sank into the rocker to Souter's left. For a few minutes the two watched the road and the birds and clouds in a companionable silence.

Finally Souter said, "I hear you got your hands full."

"Overflowing," Peller replied. "Two nutcases at once. I don't think Howard County has ever seen anything quite like it."

Souter waved that away with a dry laugh. "Lots of nutcases around here. Just most of 'em don't whack people."

Peller laughed.

"I don't guess you can talk about it, though, huh?"

"Not much, no."

"How 'bout your son? You hear from him lately?"

Peller shook his head. "Last time he called was about a month ago. I'll call him tonight, maybe."

Souter stretched his legs and adjusted himself in the rocker. "Best do that. He'll be worried."

"About what?"

"You. You're hunting dangerous game."

"I doubt he's even heard about it."

Souter fixed Peller with a jaded expression. "Son, the whole country's gonna hear about this one."

"So you heard the press conference?" the detective asked. Souter must have. When Morris had revealed that there was "an apparent pattern in the murders based on the Fibonacci series," it took only a heartbeat for the *Baltimore Sun's* reporter to ask if that meant a serial killer was on the loose. "It would seem so," the Captain had replied. That would surely set the stage for national coverage of the crimes.

But Souter replied, "What press conference?", leaving Peller to wonder how he'd known the case was that big. Then again, it was hard to put one over on Jerry. He'd been around too long, seen too much.

"You'll hear about it soon enough," Peller told him.

$$\Sigma$$

While Peller was talking with Souter, Montufar received a phone call. The caller had asked for Peller, but as he wasn't there it had been routed to her desk.

"I'm glad he figured it out."

Montufar had difficulty making out the speaker's thin, raspy voice. She wondered if it was being electronically processed or disguised in some other way. "I beg your pardon?"

"Peller," the voice whispered. "He figured out my name. I'm glad."

Montufar pushed back from her desk, stunned. The caller could only be Leo. But this wasn't how he worked. Leo sent notes, he didn't make phone calls. But no mention of the name had been made in the press conference. Only Leo would know the link between the name and the numbers.

"Are you still there?" he asked.

Montufar found her voice. "Yes, I'm here. What do you want me to do?"

"I want you to take a message for Peller."

"Okay." She grabbed a pen and a pad of large sticky notes. "What's the message?"

Dry as autumn leaves, the voice murmured, "It happens on the third floor."

She wrote and waited, but for a moment heard nothing more than the faint sound of his breathing. "What happens on the third floor?"

"You know," he said and hung up.

Montufar bit her lip. Three. The next number in the series, but with a totally different meaning than anything that went before and no possible way to know where to look. The third floor of *what?*

Snatching up the note, Montufar hurried to Morris' office and found the Captain on her way out. "I'm late for a meeting with Jeffries and Baldwin," she said, naming the Chief of Police and the Howard County Executive. "They're already getting hammered by the press. The reporters must've run straight to Baldwin's house after they got done with me. Nobody waits for Monday anymore."

"You'll want to know this," Montufar said, handing over the note. "He called, Whitney. I talked to him."

Morris gave the note a look of disgust, as though she were holding a roadkill skunk. "He doesn't call. You sure it was him?"

"Positive. He knew we'd figured out the name."

Handing the note back, Morris shook her head. "All right. Any point in setting up for a trace in case he calls again?"

"I doubt it. He's too smart for that. He didn't give me much chance to draw him out. You want me to call Rick?"

The Captain nodded. "Tell him, but there's no point in hauling him back here. This doesn't tell us anything we didn't already know. I have to go."

Returning to her desk, Montufar sank into her chair, set the note before her, and stared at it, mind racing. She disassembled every known element of the murders, then twisted and turned and pounded them into place like pieces of a poorly-cut jigsaw puzzle. No picture emerged. Why the third floor? The numbers were not random; why would their meanings be?

Frightened, frustrated, and exhausted, she leaned back in her chair and closed her eyes. In the back of her mind, her father's voice whispered reassuringly, "You can do this. You're smarter than anyone I know." But she didn't feel very smart at the moment, and all the while Leo was laughing at their inability.

Then a different voice entered her thoughts. "Pray."

That was always her mother's answer, no matter which of life's problems assailed them. Lost dogs and lost toys that returned, lost grandparents that didn't. *Pray.* In her mind's eye her mother held a rosary.

I've forgotten how to pray, Mamá.

Her mother's voice was calm and certain. *No one forgets how to pray.*

Disturbed, Montufar sat forward again, shaking off the vision, and called Peller's cellphone. When he answered, she related the news.

"It does tell us one thing new," Peller said after digesting the information. "It tells us what three means."

"But does that really mean anything? I can't see any pattern. Zero victims, one shot, firstborn son, two victims with two shots, third floor. There should be a pattern. I *want* there to be a pattern. But what if there isn't?"

"Victims, shots, birth order, then victims and shots together, then floor number. Next would be five. Five victims or shots or both?"

Montufar shuddered. In the silence that followed, something else occurred to her. "Why is Leo so interested in talking to you? He addressed all his letters to you and asked for you when he called. He even said he was glad *you* had figured out his name."

"Good question. A personal contest, maybe? His wits against mine? But why me instead of you or Eric or even Whitney?"

Glad for a different puzzle, Montufar turned it over in her mind, hoping Peller wouldn't grow impatient with the silence. Dead air in phone conversations made most people edgy. But he said nothing.

"I can think of two possibilities," she said at last. "One, he knows you personally. Two, he got your name from a news article. There are other ways he could have gotten your name, but they would more random. If nothing else, Leo's deliberate."

"I'll ponder that. Let me know if anything else happens."

Once she was off the phone, Montufar leaned on her desk and cradled her head in her hands. Had she been wrong? She had thought that once Leo knew they had worked out the numbers, the game would change. But it hadn't. He'd merely provided them with another clue like the ones gone before. The phone call had been a surprise, but it probably was his way of making sure he communicated his next move before the inevitable pranksters muddied the waters with bogus letters and phone calls. Something about Leo was evading her, something important. There was a gaping hole in her mental picture of him.

Her father's encouragement echoed in her mind once more. She wished she could talk to him. He had a way of helping her step back, see the larger patterns in whatever problems confronted her. But he had been slipping into the fog of Alzheimer's for the past year and a half. Most of the time, he didn't even know who she was.

That was the last thing Montufar wanted to think about. Focus, she told herself, but on something other than Leo. Rising, she rushed to Dumas' desk, where she found him poring over reports on the earliest of the golf attacks.

He looked up at her swift approach. "Now what?"

"I'm hungry," she said. "Let's get something to eat."

He glanced at the time on his computer. "Okay. What sounds good?"

"Chinese." Turning to go, she waved her hand behind her toward the desktop. "Bring those along. You can tell me what you found."

"I can tell you right now," he said. "Absolutely nothing." But he gathered up the papers and followed, as she knew he would.

Chapter 6

A significant aspect of mathematical research is the search for patterns. Some mathematicians spend their whole lives doing little else, with varying degrees of success. Humans like to think there are patterns everywhere, and our success is largely based on the amazing ability of our brains to tease out even the most esoteric of patterns.

But sometimes they do the job too well. Have you ever looked at the random bumps on a stucco wall and suddenly seen a human face looking back at you? You've found a pattern in the noise, but it's a meaningless pattern, a random happenstance. It was not put there intentionally.

The trick, it turns out, is not merely to find patterns, but to find meaningful patterns. There are times when it is very hard to know the difference. Σ

"The first four attacks tell us very little," Dumas told Montufar around a forkful of General Tso's chicken. His taste buds couldn't be happier. This was one of his favorite dishes, done to tangy perfection by one of the best Chinese restaurants in the state of Maryland, a place that to outward seeming was just a hole-in-the-wall, a smallish storefront on the end of a smallish strip mall tucked into a wooded corner a block off the main road. It couldn't seat more than about a dozen people, yet each bite the chefs served up was exquisite bliss, seducing the palate with flavors bold or subtle as suited each dish.

Unlike Montufar, Dumas hadn't mastered the use of chopsticks and had no desire to try. He twirled the bit of chicken on his fork, gazing at it lovingly even as he set forth the facts in the case.

"First was Chelsea MacIntyre, age thirty-four, married with two children. Clobbered in the parking lot of the Dorsey's Search Village Center. She had backed into a space along the outer edge of the parking lot under a line of trees. She was putting her purchases into the trunk when she was struck from behind. She didn't see the attacker, but saw what she thought was the head of a golf club, an iron, on the ground in front of her before she blacked out. Her money, necklace, earrings, and wedding band were stolen."

Montufar seemed more intent on her plate of shrimp with lobster sauce than his narrative, but he knew she was taking it all in.

"Second, Latasha Childress, age twenty, college student. She parked her car by the tennis courts at the southeast corner of Centennial Park and went for a jog around the lake. She left her purse and laptop computer in the car. When she got back, she was struck from behind while unlocking her car door. Her money and laptop were stolen. She remembers seeing a man walking away from her with a golf club over his shoulder before the attack, while she was still approaching her car. He looked like a soldier with a gun. Her words. But she can't be sure he was the one who attacked her, and she didn't see his face."

"He took her computer? That's not his usual style," Montufar said.

"I think it tells us he's after valuables that are easily liquidated," Dumas replied. "He could have driven off with her car—or by now, several cars. But he's mostly gone after cash and jewelry. The laptop happened to be there, so why not?"

He paused to enjoy a few bites before continuing.

"Third, Juana Rojas, age forty-seven, is an attorney married to a cardiologist. They live in a *very* nice house on the other side of Clarksville Pike from the park. She was all dressed up and ready to go to a party at the home of one of her well-heeled friends, but while she was opening the door of her SUV she was savagely attacked from behind. She received multiple head wounds—including one that fractured her skull— plus bruises on her back and left side. Far more than was necessary to just incapacitate her. She didn't see the golf club, but her wounds were consistent with those on the previous victims, so we think there's good reason to suspect the mad golfer again."

Montufar looked up suddenly. "He was angry," she said, sounding surprised.

"Apparently."

"No, Eric. This guy was furious. But the victims' descriptions of the golfer don't agree. Remember what Bess Williams said? He was whistling as he walked away. Why would the same man be so furious with Juana Rojas?" She frowned. "Is there a copycat out there? Or was it just because she's rich...?"

"...And he's not," Dumas finished. "Makes sense. And she had a lot on her person just then, particularly some very pricey jewelry. All stolen, along with her cash."

Montufar put down her fork, half of her lunch untouched. A scowl darkened her face. Dumas watched her for a time, visualizing the wheels turning in her head. What was she seeing that he wasn't? But she said nothing further, so he moved on.

"And fourth, Lisa Hyeung, age twenty-eight, a nurse working third shift at the University of Maryland Medical Center. Clubbed while sitting by the lake reading a book in the early morning, a spot she frequented to unwind after work. She must've been a disappointment to him, because she didn't have much on her, just a bit of cash. She was wearing a cheap ring. It was found on the ground near her. He must have realized it wasn't worth his time after he took it off her hand. Again, she saw nothing, but the wound was consistent with the previous attacks."

Dumas saw in Montufar's eyes that something else had clicked, but she hesitated long enough for him to wonder if he'd been wrong. He waited anyway.

Finally she said, "The double murder. Rick said there was a ring on the ground. A cheap ring. It had belonged to the woman. He also said it looked like mud had been kicked onto her."

"You're suggesting Leo killed her and took her ring, but got mad when he saw it wasn't worth much? So he threw it down and kicked mud on her?"

She nodded, but hesitantly. "It sounds plausible. But I don't know. It doesn't feel right."

"Yeah…" Leo, Dumas knew, was devious. He'd carefully planned the murders to correspond with a mathematical sequence, yet had altered the details of each crime to prevent the appearance of any pattern. If he was also the golfer, then he had assumed a very different personality for those attacks. Dumas thought it just possible. Both crime sequences had an element of lunacy to them.

So the one time Leo decides to rob a murder victim, it turns out she's wearing a worthless trinket—another worthless trinket. And the carefully concealed rage that had exploded during the robbery of the wealthy Juana Rojas once again rises to the surface.

But he found another possibility. "You know," he told Montufar, "even if the murders and the robberies are done by different people, this suggests there could be a connection between them. Maybe Leo is trying to throw us off the track. He knows what the golfer has done in considerable detail, and uses one of those details to confuse us."

Montufar nodded thoughtfully. "Or to tip us off. He told me he was glad that we'd figured out his name. Maybe he wants us to know that he knows all about the golfer, too."

"This is getting way too twisted," Dumas said.

"And it'll probably get even more twisted before we understand it."

Which Dumas did not particularly want to think about.

Σ

While his colleagues dined, Peller broiled himself a cheeseburger and complemented it with a side of store-bought potato salad. He moved mechanically through preparation, consumption, and clean-up. Typically this was the time of day Sandra would slip quietly into his thoughts. Some evenings her presence there would be like a comforting embrace. Others, her physical absence would threaten to overwhelm him. But this evening, she seemed more a silent companion, letting him know he wasn't alone but giving him space as he mentally picked through the details of the murders, seeking some hidden commonality that might tell him where the next victim would die.

Nothing.

He threw some laundry in to wash and tuned the TV to the news. Alongside the usual fires, robberies, and rampant unemployment, the police press conference from Howard County got top billing. Peller found it hard to judge the coverage the way the average viewer might, but he thought the Captain made it look like her detectives knew what they were doing in spite of the efforts of the gathered reporters to find a chink in her armor.

After the news, he retreated to his den. Feeling as though Sandra was close at his side, he looked through his collection of books: largely history and science fiction with an occasional western thrown in for good measure. Nothing sounded interesting tonight. He sat in an easy chair and stared blankly at the telephone that sat on the table next to him. The clock was just kissing six in Denver—a tad early, but maybe Jason would be home.

He picked up the phone and dialed. On the third ring, a young voice chirped, "Hello!"

Peller smiled. "Well, hi there, Susie."

"Grandpa! Grandpa!"

In the background he heard a bit of squealing followed by a distant, "I wanna talk!"

"How are you today?"

"I'm good! Guess what? Yesterday at school a fireman came to our class!"

Leaning back, Peller immersed himself in his eight-year-old granddaughter's chatter for several minutes. Eventually she finished her recitation of exciting things that had happened, said goodbye, and relinquished the phone to her younger brother.

"Hi, Grandpa!"

"Hi, Andrew! What's new with you?"

"A fireman came to school!"

Peller laughed. The six-year-old was known to mimic his sister. "The same one as came to Susie's class?" he asked.

"Noooooo! Ours was tall!"

"Now how do you know that?"

"Well, 'cause I saw them go by the window. There was lots of them!"

By the time Andrew had finished his stories of firemen at school, Peller was convinced that the whole department had been there. Eventually the youngster said goodbye, and Jason took up the phone.

"Hi, Dad. I hear you have some excitement out your way."

"A couple of nutcases," Peller replied, trying to sound noncommittal.

Jason said nothing for a moment, as though he were waiting for elaboration, then he changed the subject. "Belinda lost her job today. Her company laid off two hundred fifty people."

Peller exhaled heavily. His daughter-in-law had worked in marketing for a large telecom equipment manufacturer. Last he'd heard, she'd been in line for promotion to management. "How's she taking it?"

"About as well as anyone. She's already circulating her resumé, but with this economy it's going to take some time to find anything."

"You okay for money?"

"For the moment. At least my job is stable, and we don't have too much debt."

"Let me know if you need any help," Peller said, then after a pause he added, "I could come out there."

"You've got your hands full there, Dad."

It might have been Peller's imagination, but he thought Jason had said it a bit too quickly. "This won't last too much longer," he said. "Once we have these lunatics locked up . . ."

He let the sentence hang.

So did Jason. Then, "We can talk about it when that happens. I don't think even you can predict how long it will take to catch them."

"I suppose you're right. Well then, all of you take care of yourselves. I'll be thinking of you."

"We'll be thinking of you, too, Dad. Please be careful."

"I will," he promised.

∑

Sometime around three in the morning on Sunday, March sixth, on the third floor of the third building of the Cedar Forest apartment complex, a woman died when gas fumes from four unlit stove burners opened full throttle filled her apartment. An anonymous call to 911 made from within the apartment itself alerted emergency responders to the incident, but they arrived too late to do anything more than prevent an explosion and further casualties.

They also found another hint that the woman's death was not an accident: a note scrawled in an almost illegible hand. After a bit of mutual consultation and a lot of eyestrain, the investigating team deciphered it as: "Ask Peller if he got my message."

∑

"When I get done with him," Peller muttered, "he won't have any use for a lawyer."

Montufar put a hand on his shoulder and squeezed. "Don't go psycho on me," she said. "We have enough psychos running around as it is."

They stood in the parking lot in front of the building, one of four three-story units nestled in a heavily-wooded tract of land between Cedar Lane and the eastern end of Hobbit's Glen Golf Course. From the outside the buildings were neat and trim, with new vinyl siding and undulating ribbons of landscape plants that were no doubt lush and vibrant in the summer. In contrast to the mood, the sky overhead was cloudless and bright, with the sun on the rise in the southeast.

Seven forty-five, Peller had noted on the car clock before they got out. Four hours and forty five minutes ago, the apartment just above where he now stood was filled with gas and a woman had died. A woman with a name and a family and a life. Lorna Bigelow, age 87, African-American, widow, mother, grandmother, great-grandmother, descendant of slaves, a writer of some modest note who had explored the history of Catholicism and slavery in the U.S. through both fiction and nonfiction. Peller wasn't familiar with her writing, but Montufar had dug up the information somewhere.

And now Bigelow was dead for one and only one reason: she had lived on the third floor.

The detectives went inside, up the stairs, and into the apartment. It was modest and clean, furnished in swirling blues and purples and darkish woods. A faint scent of mercaptan lingered in the air, perhaps absorbed by the fabric of sofas and chairs, now slowly being released again. Nothing was out of place. The note had been found on the kitchen counter beside the wall phone that had been used to make the call. The crime scene unit had meticulously gone over the place, but Peller knew they would come up with little or nothing. Leo was too smart and too careful.

This, Peller thought, *is a waste of time.* "We'll need to listen to the 911 call when we get back," he told Montufar. But he knew that that, too, would be practically worthless.

She gazed at him for a moment, her eyes concerned. "You sound like you're about ready to give up."

Evading her observation, he said, "We know what happened here, at least basically. Leo gained entry after Bigelow was asleep, turned on the gas, and called 911. Then he left. And here we are, on the third floor. We also know what comes next. Five. But one crucial element remains, and I don't know how to find it."

"What five means?"

He shook his head and went to the window, which looked out onto the wooded lot behind the building. The golf course lay beyond the bare trees, empty of golfers mad or otherwise. A flock of starlings descended into the treetops, chattering loudly. "No. Why he's doing this."

Montufar joined him at the window. "Yeah. The numbers don't tell us that. They're just a vehicle."

"But for what? He's been silent about it."

"Maybe. . ."

Peller glanced at her. She was frowning at the world beyond, but he knew she wasn't seeing it. Her vision was focused within, on ideas chasing through her mind like—if it wasn't too fanciful an image for such grave circumstances—a litter of puppies.

After giving her a few moments, he prompted her: "You've thought of something."

She nodded. "What if the numbers are not the only pattern here?"

"He's avoided all semblance of pattern, Corina. You know that."

"I'm not saying I can see it, but think about it. The numbers follow a fixed pattern, but if he hadn't pointed us to Fibonacci, we wouldn't have realized it, at least not so quickly." She turned to face him, her eyes intense. "The numbers mean things: how many victims, how many shots fired." She gestured at the room. "What floor the victim lives on. We can't see any pattern in those things yet, but maybe it's there."

Peller's first inclination was to dismiss the thought, but he hesitated. Montufar's intuitions tended towards the uncanny. "Could be," he replied. "But how many people have to die before we do see it?"

"I think maybe we need to get some outside help."

Very little Montufar said surprised him anymore, but this did. Like most detectives he knew, she usually thought she could handle the cases assigned to her without consulting outsiders. "What sort of help?" He almost expected her answer to involve priests or psychics.

He could tell she was purposely avoiding his gaze. "Someone whose job involves analyzing patterns. We need a mathematician."

Chapter 7

I had heard of the killings but paid little attention to them. Polignac's conjecture, a proposition of which you have likely not heard dealing with prime numbers, occupied much of my thought at that time, so much so that mundane affairs largely passed me by. But when the case was set before me, it seemed just intriguing enough to catch my notice.

It is perhaps fortunate that we cannot always see the end in the beginning. Σ

Captain Morris had arrived at headquarters just before the detectives did and now listened to Montufar's proposal with her eyes fixed on the ceiling. "Are you sure this will help?" she asked.

"No," Montufar admitted. "But it might, and I don't see how it can hurt."

Her gaze descended to meet Montufar's. "I have to show you something first. This arrived in yesterday's mail." She handed an envelope across the desk.

Peller rubbed his eyes. "Another note from Leo?"

"No."

Montufar examined the envelope. "Typed," she said. "No stamp, no return address. Addressed to you, not Rick. Hand-delivered?"

Morris shrugged. "It was in the incoming mail, but didn't come through the post office."

Montufar opened it and read aloud from the enclosed page. "Dear Howard County Police. You may know the pattern, but you don't know where I will strike next. I will go on killing for as long as I like and you can't stop me. So you may as well write parking tickets instead of wasting your time on me. P.S. You can start calling me Scorpio. It's a fitting name." She put the note down and muttered, "Jerk."

Peller shook his head. "Why do they do it?"

"To see if they can make the evening news," Morris said. "The point is, you're going to have to be careful what you feed your professor. We want him chewing on the good meat, not the rancid stuff."

"Fortunately," Peller said, "we know Leo well enough by now. This doesn't even come close."

Σ

The call seemed straightforward enough:

"Howard County 911, what's your emergency?"

"We have a serious gas leak here."

"How many people are in the area?"

"Just two of us. Me and my mother. I think she's passed out."

"Okay, I have your address here."

While the dispatcher confirmed the address with the caller, Montufar told Peller, "That's him. It's the same voice as the guy I talked to."

"You're calling from an apartment?"

"Yes."

"Can you get your mother out?"

"I don't think so."

"Okay, get yourself out of there. Emergency units and BGE are on their way."

"Please hurry. If this place blows up, more than one person will be hurt."

"Yes, sir. Just get yourself out of there."

Peller pushed back from his desk as the recording playing on his computer ended. "That's an odd way of phrasing it. 'More than one person.'"

"He didn't want anyone other than his chosen victim to get hurt."

Peller thought there was a bit more question in her voice than usual. "Why would he care? The number didn't refer to the body count this time."

"It never has, except once. Otherwise, there has only been one victim at a time."

Captain Morris dropped a slip of paper in front of Peller. "Here's your mathematician," she said. "Tomio Kaneko. Answers to Tom, so I'm told. Friend of a friend of a friend. He teaches at Hopkins in the city. Given the urgency of the matter, he agreed to meet you in his office this afternoon at three."

Peller nodded his thanks, and in Morris's wake Dumas slipped in. "What are you doing here on a Sunday?" Peller asked.

"I was called in," Dumas said, more cheerfully than Peller would have expected. "We got a tip on the sketch of the golfer. A guy who says he knows who it is. Can you spare Corina?"

The two rushed out, leaving Peller on his own, but it didn't last. Not more than a minute later the phone rang. Absently he took up the receiver. "Peller."

Two seconds of silence elapsed. Then Peller heard the faint whisper of breathing: once, twice, three times. His patience ran out before the fourth exhale, and he snapped, "What do you want?"

"Ah, it is you," the voice whispered. "Did you get my note?"

A monstrous realization suddenly loomed within Peller's mind. "Who is this?"

"The note I left on the third floor. Did you get it?"

Peller sprang to his feet and motioned wildly to Morris with his free hand, trying to get her attention, but she was focused on her computer. "Yes, I got it."

"Good. I presume the answer is yes."

He had to think a moment before he remembered. The note had asked if he had gotten the message left by phone with Montufar. "Yes," he said, "it is."

Morris finally looked up from her computer. "It's him?" she asked, more by gesture than by voice. Peller nodded, and she came to stand by his desk.

"I'm going to give you the next two numbers now," the caller said, "so pay attention. Building number five. And finally, a gathering of eight."

Peller wrote the message down verbatim while Morris read over his shoulder. She leaned heavily on the desk and muttered, "Christ."

"Understood," Peller said, struggling to keep anger out of his voice.

"Until next time, then," the caller said.

Before the connection was broken, Peller demanded, "Why me?"

Leo's breathing came heavier, sounded less controlled. For a full five seconds there was no other sound, then connection was cut.

Peller replaced the receiver. "Damn," he said. "He does know me."

Σ

Woodland Road bounded the eastern end of Centennial Park, a backbone upon which about twenty houses, mostly older bungalows, huddled in a clearing in the woods on the west side of the road along a series of unnamed drives. Between the curves and forks in the road and the curious angles at which some of the houses had been built, the area looked to Dumas like a playground where a huge set of building blocks had been dumped and forgotten by a giant child.

The witness lived in one of the houses that backed up against the trees of the park. It was a smallish place painted a light tan with white shutters and a less-than-new Honda Civic in the driveway. He was leaning against the car talking on his cell phone when the detectives drove up. As they approached him, he said into the phone, "That's why I say you're an idiot. I'll do what I can, but this is the last time. The cops are here. I gotta go."

Dumas and Montufar watched expressionlessly as he snapped the phone shut and shoved it in his left pants pocket. A big man, clean-shaven with close-cropped hair, he smiled as though embarrassed that they'd heard what he'd said.

"A younger and less experienced cousin," he explained. "Always getting into trouble." He thrust his hand toward Dumas, who grasped it and shook. The guy was strong. "Luke Frey." He offered his hand to Montufar with less force.

The detectives introduced themselves as Frey gave Montufar a measured once-over. "You seem familiar," he said.

"Can't say I recall you," she replied blandly.

Dumas barely managed to avoid cracking a smile. Montufar had a knack for deflecting come-ons in a way that left men wondering whether or not they'd been insulted.

Frey seemed to like it, though. "One of my special skills," he said with a laugh. "I guess you guys want to talk business. Come on inside."

He led them through the front door and into a plain-looking living room furnished with a tan sofa, a few wooden chairs, and a couple of unpretentious end tables. The walls were strangely bare except for a photograph of an elderly man and woman. Dumas noted a clear family resemblance between Frey and the man.

They sat, and Montufar handed Frey a copy of the sketch of the golfer. He studied it for a moment then said, "Definitely him."

"Where did you see him?" Dumas asked.

"Right here in my backyard, if you can believe it. Two days ago, about nine-thirty, ten o'clock in the morning. I was in the kitchen, in the back of the house, cleaning up after breakfast. I looked out the window just as this guy comes out of the woods, traipses across my yard, and walks down the street. Yesterday I saw the sketch on the news and realized it was him."

"Do you remember what he was wearing?"

Frey nodded. "Yeah. He had on a trench coat. Like that old TV detective. Columbo."

Dumas glanced at Montufar. She nodded. They both knew what must have happened. After robbing Regina Collins the golfer had cut back into the woods, crossed the park, and come out here. But on his way to where?

Montufar put the question to Frey.

He leaned back with a look of concentration. "Well, I think he must live right here in this neighborhood,. You got a handful of houses here, and a few more off Columbia Road." He motioned towards the street and a stand of trees beyond. "Just back of those trees. But if I were him, I wouldn't want to walk all day to get home. I'll bet he's right here. He's probably one of my neighbors."

"Do you know your neighbors?" Dumas asked.

"Nah. I've only lived here for about six months and I'm not the outgoing type."

The detectives stood, and Frey rose a fraction of a second after them. "We really appreciate the help, Mr. Frey," Dumas said.

He looked a bit crestfallen. "It wasn't enough, was it?"

"We'll know soon enough. At any rate, aside from the sketch it's the best information we've gotten so far."

That seemed to cheer him up. He opened the door for them and watched as they returned to their car. Montufar looked back just before she slipped into the passenger seat.

Frey grinned at her and winked. She didn't return either gesture.

$$\Sigma$$

The office that Peller entered in Krieger Hall—home to the Johns Hopkins University Mathematics Department—felt like a movie set. The room was immaculate. Regimented books stood in their appointed squads on the wall-to-wall book-shelves. The professor's bare white desk was occupied only by a mail sorter, its papers stacked precisely, and a single computer carefully angled to allow easy access without obstructing the view of the door. No photographs or other personal touches marred the cool expanse. The lone window that looked out on the quad showed a meticulous-ly-manicured lawn tastefully dotted with trees. Neither leaf nor blade of grass was misaligned. Peller wondered if the landscapers had been ordered to make the view outside as perfect as the one inside.

Behind the desk, Tomio Kaneko was hard at work, typing on the computer. A man of average height and slight build, Peller guessed he was in his mid-sixties. With-out taking his eyes off the monitor, he motioned Peller in. The detective sat in one of the two chairs facing the desk and waited.

"Good afternoon, Lieutenant Peller," Kaneko said, still focused on the com-puter. "Please call me Tom."

"And you can call me Rick," Peller replied. "I didn't expect to find you work-ing. I hope I'm not interrupting anything important."

Kaneko shook his head. "Unfortunately, even mathematicians serve the bu-reaucracy. I took the opportunity to work on this report while waiting for you. But I can stop here." He finished typing and made some final adjustments to the computer; then, folding his hands on his desk, he turned to face his guest. His gaze was intense enough to make Peller uncomfortable. "I understand there is numerically-inclined murderer on the loose."

Peller nodded. "We know he's using the Fibonacci series as a basis for the crimes, but unfortunately the numbers are attached to something different every time, and we can't anticipate his moves because the information he feeds us is minimal."

"Tell me about them." Kaneko took a blank sheet of paper from one of his bins and picked up a pencil.

"First was zero, nobody dies. Then a murder with one shot fired, then the killing of a firstborn son, then two victims killed with two shots, then a killing on the third floor of an apartment building. The last one was done by flooding the apartment with gas from an unlit stove."

Kaneko, who had been making a list, looked up, clearly disturbed, but said nothing.

"He phoned in the next two numbers this morning."

"Five and eight."

"Yes. Building number five and a gathering of eight."

"I see." The mathematician wrote down those items and studied the list. "Victims, shots, birth order. Victims, building floor, building number. Victims. This could be a pattern, but if so it can't go on much longer."

"Why not?"

Kaneko shifted in his chair. "Because it would become nightmarish very quickly. As you have learned from your research, each number in the Fibonacci sequence is the sum of the previous two. If every third number is a number of victims, then the next two numbers signifying the number of victims would be thirty-four, followed by one hundred forty-four."

Peller mulled that over for a moment. "So you don't think that's a real pattern."

"No. At least, I hope not. Thousands can be slaughtered at one time. Terrorists have done so, and governments have done so. My father died when the atomic bomb was dropped on Nagasaki. But those kinds of killings are not mathematically precise, Rick. A mind that is set on killing according to this kind of sequence must demand precision. How do you kill exactly one hundred forty-four people?"

"Good point," Peller said. And then he remembered the phone call and a small detail he had written down but not thought about. "Wait a minute. The sequence ends with eight. Leo told me that. He said 'finally.'"

"Leo?" Kaneko said.

"That's what he calls himself. Sort of. Variations on Leonardo of Pisa. That's how we figured out he was using the Fibonacci series. Anyway, he didn't just say, 'A gathering of eight.' He said, 'And *finally*, a gathering of eight.'"

"So you think he will stop killing, then?"

No, Peller thought, not Leo. This was another part of his sick game. After eight, something else happens, something not in keeping with the pattern he had so carefully built up.

But then he had another thought. Maybe Leo wasn't really a serial killer at all. Maybe this gathering of eight had been his real target all along. But if so, why the other murders? *To see if they can make the evening news,* he could almost hear Captain Morris saying. But that didn't sit well with Peller. Leo was after something, but it wasn't publicity. He would have bet his house on that.

"Listen, Tom. Can you pay us a visit? We can give you access to everything about the case. My partner, Corina Montufar, is convinced there is some pattern we are not seeing, some kind of mathematical pattern more than just the Fibonacci numbers. Maybe when you have all the information at your disposal you'll see something we can't see."

"Of course," Kaneko replied quietly. He leaned back in his chair and fixed Peller with the stare of a professor waiting for a slow student to work out an answer. "I can come tomorrow."

Chapter 8

My initial impression of Rick Peller was that of simple effi-
ciency. It seemed to me he had identified the key to the problem facing
him and was focused on understanding that key and how it might be
used to best effect. Of course, this was a mathematician's understanding
of the matter. I had no experience of how crimes are solved, nor of the
messy entanglements that complicate that endeavor. Σ

For Montufar, Monday morning lay in ruins before it started, destroyed by a
barrage of unforeseeable events. Within seconds of her alarm waking her at five-thirty,
her sister Ella called, crying so hysterically that it took Montufar several minutes to
calm her down enough to learn that their brother Eduardo had been in a five-car pileup
and the EMTs had airlifted him to the University of Maryland Medical Center's shock
trauma unit. Montufar said she'd be there as fast as she could, but before she could
finish dressing the phone went off again. Expecting it to be Ella again, she answered
with a quick, "Yes?"

It was Peller. "Bad news," he said. "A murder's been reported in the south
part of the county, off of Clarkesville Road about a mile north of Highland. The address is five MacKenzie Farm Road. The number five. It has to be Leo again."

"Rick," she said, but he didn't wait.

"We have to get right on it. The victim was Roger Harrison."

She bit her lip, trying to think, but her mind was a whirl. The name was familiar, but she couldn't quite place it.

"State senator Roger Harrison," Peller said.

"Oh, hell." She sat on the edge of the bed and pinched her eyes shut.

"You want me to pick you up?"

She swallowed, hard enough for him to hear, she was sure. "My brother was
in an accident this morning. He's in the hospital. I was about to go there." Peller said
nothing for a moment, so without enthusiasm she added, "I suppose I could meet you
down there. I wouldn't have to stay long at the hospital."

"I'll handle it, Corina," he told her. "Go take care of your brother." Before she could reply, he hung up as though not wanting to give her a chance to object.

I don't have time to think about it, she told herself, and quickly finished dressing, grabbed her purse and rushed out to her car. As she slipped the key into the ignition, her cell phone went off. Dumas, she noted. *Now what?*

"You're not going to believe this," he said. "We almost caught him last night."

"The golfer?"

"Yeah. Frey was right. He was living three streets away. The officers doing the canvass knocked on the door, he opened it—and as they held up the sketch to ask if he knew the guy in the picture, they realized it was him. He slammed the door in their faces and took off. The door was locked, and by the time they got in, he was headed out the back door into the woods. They pursued him, but before they could close in, he shot both of them."

"Oh, no." Montufar had an instant mental image of them on life support.

"Not seriously," Dumas added quickly. "One of them caught it in the leg and the other in the shoulder and hip. They'll be okay, but it sure ended the chase in a hurry."

"No idea where he went?"

"Nope. But we know who he is now. His name's Julian Szwiec, age twenty-two, a high school dropout who's worked a string of low-end jobs and is currently unemployed. We don't know much else about him yet, but we should by this afternoon. Whitney is going to hold a press conference at ten this morning to release the name. She'd like us to be there."

Montufar rubbed her eyes. Just what she needed. "My brother was in a car accident this morning. I'm just leaving for the hospital."

"Oh, hey, I'm really sorry," Dumas said, his voice quieter. "You need any help? I can stop by if you want."

"I'll be okay. Just let the Captain know. I'll call in when I know more."

She drove to the hospital in a mental fog, unable to sort out anything. The oldest child in their family, Eduardo had given them much of their strength through his cheerful outlook and his belief that they could accomplish anything they put their minds to. Of all her siblings, he was the one who had faithfully kept their family's

Catholic heritage, trusting in God to carry them all through the changes and chances of life.

Montufar didn't see herself as dependent upon him, but she had to admit that there had been a few times when she might not have made it without him to cheer her on. Her first year at the academy had nearly been a disaster. The physical rigors of the training, sometimes almost beyond her strength, had left her exhausted and depressed, and more than once she'd been harassed by instructors and fellow cadets on account of her gender, her ethnicity, or both. Eduardo had always been there to keep her focused.

"Someday," he'd told her time and again, "all these fools will look up to you. They're gonna be ashamed of themselves, then." And there were, indeed, a few officers who couldn't quite look her in the eye.

Arriving at the hospital, she parked and rushed to the emergency room. The waiting area was only a quarter full and relatively quiet. A slight woman with a pale, bony face and raven hair rocked an infant in her arms. The woman seemed barely out of childhood herself. She sat alone, and Montufar wondered if she were one of the myriad teenagers who, unwarned by wiser and older women, had fallen into the trap of some man's lie. The baby lay still in its blankets, and Montufar hoped that the child was ill, not dying, not dead. In Montufar's overwrought imagination the scene became a grotesque mixture of the Nativity and the Pietà.

A few seats to the mother's left, an elderly black man with a stony gaze held his wife's hand while she whispered at him nonstop. It was impossible to tell which of them, if either, needed medical attention. Montufar closed her eyes as if by doing so she could close her mind's eye as well.

"Corina!"

Montufar's eyes snapped open. Her sister Ella, the youngest of her clan, was seated along a wall, waving frantically to her. The note of hysteria remained in her voice. Montufar slipped into the seat next to her and Ella threw herself into her sister's arms.

"It's all right; I'm here," Montufar said soothingly. "Where's Eduardo?"

Ella loosened her grip but kept her face cradled on Montufar's shoulder. "In surgery. He fractured his skull and pelvis and I don't know what else."

"Do you know what happened?"

Ella shook her head. "Just that he was driving to work and there was an accident with five cars. He got hit from the left." She choked back a sob. "First mom, then dad, now Eduardo. What are we going to do, Corina? "

Montufar took her sister by the shoulders, pushed her back so they could look in each other's eyes, and squeezed gently. "What Eduardo would want us to do. Keep hope alive."

Ella wiped away her tears with the back of her hand and nodded.

"We have each other, and anyway, he's going to be fine."

Ella looked away. "You don't know that. He could have some kind of brain injury."

"Ella, look at me," Montufar said firmly. Their eyes met again. "Have faith."

Ella let go of Montufar and fished in her handbag for a tissue. "That's..."

"What Mom used to tell us. I know."

Ella wiped her eyes. Giving Montufar a sidelong glance, she said, "Not what you usually say, though."

Montufar shrugged. "Things haven't been usual. I was thinking about her the other day, and dad, too. Eduardo is more like them than either of us, but they are in us, too. Their faith in us, it's their gift to us. We just have to remember."

Ella nodded. "I'll try. You were always stronger than me. But I'll try."

Σ

MacKenzie Farm Road was a cul-de-sac as much in the middle of nowhere as one could get in central Maryland, which wasn't much to Peller's way of thinking, but he supposed people liked to think they were getting away from it all. Most were large affairs no more than ten years old built on lots of half an acre or more. Number five was, perhaps curiously given who had lived here, smaller than the rest but looked newer. A two story house with a half-bricked façade and pale blue vinyl siding, it sported a three-car garage and was surrounded by azaleas and tufts of tallish ornamental grasses which had turned brown for the winter and needed to be cut back.

Roger Harrison, a state senator serving his second term, had been reasonably well-liked by the people of his district. Peller knew he was one of the more vocal politicians calling for fiscal restraint in the face of growing deficits, but otherwise he wasn't sure what the man stood for. As of this morning, it was a moot point. Whatever causes he might have espoused, it would now be up to others to pursue them.

It should have been a typical day: the senator was preparing to drive his teenage daughter Paula to high school and then go on to a meeting with some local business owners. Instead, he had been taken out with one shot to the head. Neighbors rushed from their homes to find his body sprawled on the concrete halfway between the door and the car and Paula collapsed to her knees, screaming.

When Peller arrived on the scene, the crime scene unit had cordoned off the area and a pair of EMTs hovered over Paula. "Take it easy on her," one of them warned Peller. "We're moving her to the hospital as soon as you're done."

Peller crouched down in front of Paula. She had been neatly dressed in a pleated wool skirt and cardigan—her choice of wardrobe struck Peller as strangely preppie for this day and age when kids went to school in pajama pants—and her hair and face carefully groomed, but now the hem of her skirt was dirty from the driveway, her hair was shaken loose, and mascara bled down her cheeks. "Paula, do you remember what happened?"

She shook her head dumbly, her eyes vacant.

"Anything?" he prompted. "Anything at all?"

No.

"Can you tell me which way the shot came from?"

She looked up at him, eyes haunted. "I don't know," she whispered. "It was so loud. It echoed . . ." She dropped her head to stare at the ground. "Daddy . . . ."

Peller straightened up and nodded to the EMTs. The woman took her gently by the shoulders. "Come on, honey," she said in the voice mothers use to calm very small children. Peller hoped that the girl would be all right. It was unsettling to see a thousand-yard stare on the face of a sixteen-year-old.

Now Peller took a good look around, standing next to the spot where Harrison had died. There were a number of possible places the shooter could have been hiding. If not actually in one of the nearby houses—which Peller didn't think likely but was always possible—he could have been in one of seven or eight stretches of the woodland that meandered behind them. From any of them, it would have been a respectable distance.

The situation reminded Peller of the first murder. Mark Patterson, the snow-plow driver, had been killed while driving past Symphony Woods. The killer had apparently been back in the woods, a pretty fair shot as one of the officers on the scene had commented at that time, through the trees at a moving target. Harrison, too, had been the victim of a pretty fair shot. The other shootings had been done at closer range, but each victim had been shot just once.

Leo, it seemed, was at least a marksman and quite possibly a sniper. One of the killings had been done with a military weapon, which suggested he had a military background. It wasn't much, but Peller would take anything at this point.

He had dispatched officers to talk to the neighbors and wanted to stick around until they reported back. If anything interesting turned up, he would want to interview the witnesses personally. But it wasn't a day for plans to go well.

His cell phone rang with the tone he had set for Captain Morris. "We've got huge trouble," she told him.

"Worse than a dead politician?"

"Much worse. A whole family has been killed in Clarksville, in a house right next to River Hill High School."

"My God." Peller felt the need to sit down but instead stomped into the middle of the yard and glared at one of the places Leo might have earlier hidden.

"Eight people, Rick. Just like he said. A group of eight. Father, mother, grandmother, and five children."

"All shot?"

"Execution-style." Her voice sounded far away.

"How old were the kids?"

"The oldest was twenty, the youngest nine. I know Corina's at the hospital, but maybe we should..."

"No," Peller said sharply. "See if Eric can get up there, and I'll join him as soon as I finish here."

Morris let a bit of dead air hang between them. "All right. But we've got to stop this animal, Rick. We can't let this go on any longer."

"If you have any suggestions," he snapped, "I'm open to them."

In the ensuing silence Peller nearly apologized, but before he could Morris said, "I wish I did." The sorrow in her voice told him she wasn't offended, just desperate.

Across the street, one of the officers emerged from a vaguely castle-like house and motioned Peller over. "Have Eric call me if he needs anything," he told Morris. "Something might have turned up here."

He hurried to the castle-house, where the officer motioned him in. "The lady of the house, Virginia Smullyan, says she saw a man with a rifle out in the woods."

"Can she describe him?" They made their way through a high-ceilinged foyer. On the left, Peller noted a coat closet with full-mirror doors. His reflection looked more haggard than he would have thought. On the right, the walls were liberally hung with oil paintings, mostly nature scenes that might have been local: forests and rivers and one a view of the Chesapeake with the twin spans of the Bay Bridge in the far distance.

"Yeah, and I think she's got a pretty good eye," the officer told him with a gesture at the artwork. "She painted all of these."

They found her seated on a plush gray loveseat in the living room, surrounded by more overstuffed furniture in coordinating colors and a scattering of small glass tables. More of her paintings adorned the walls. She was in her mid-fifties, Peller guessed, short and a bit on the dumpy side, dressed in jeans and a t-shirt printed with stylized splatters of paint spelling the words, "Caution: Artist at work!"

Peller introduced himself, and she motioned him to the chair to her right. He felt like he was sinking into a pile of melted marshmallows.

"I'm told you saw someone," he said, pulling himself forward in an attempt to escape the furniture's smothering embrace.

"Yes, back there." She motioned towards the picture window that looked out onto the woods behind the house. "It was just after seven. The light was wonderful this morning, and it struck me that I hadn't painted anything right here, close to home. I guess I never realized what was outside my own back door. I thought I might paint our little woods here. I was sitting in that chair by the window when I saw him. He had a rifle and was standing very still just inside the edge of the woods. I thought he was a hunter. We have lots of deer around here."

"The season's over," Peller said.

"Oh. I don't know how that works."

He shrugged it off. "Did you see him take a shot?"

"No, he was just standing there, very still, watching something. I couldn't tell what, and after a moment I went on to other things. I did hear a shot maybe ten minutes later. I went back to look, but he was gone." Smullyan folded her hands in her lap and studied them. "I guess he was waiting to kill Roger. That poor family. If I'd been more suspicious, maybe I could have prevented it."

"Don't blame yourself. This guy is smart. Even if we could have gotten here in time to save Mr. Harrison, we wouldn't have caught him and he would have found another opportunity later."

She looked up, eyes wide. "Wait. Is he that Fibonacci guy I heard about on the news?"

Peller nodded.

"My God."

Not giving her a chance to think about it, Peller said, "I have two very important questions. First, can you describe him?"

Smullyan nodded confidently.

"Good. And second, is there any chance he saw you?" He rather didn't want to ask, because the implication would certainly be frightening, but he couldn't take any chances with her safety either.

But she wasn't fazed in the least. "None whatsoever. I was sitting too far back from the window. The sunlight reflecting off the glass would have kept him from seeing anything inside."

Peller relaxed. "All right. We're going to have you talk with a sketch artist, but if you can give me a quick description it will help."

She straightened and closed her eyes. "He was tall, maybe about six foot three, and big, but with a lean face. All angles. He looked fit. Maybe that's why I was thinking he was a hunter. He was clean-shaven, with a military haircut, and wearing dark jeans, a camo jacket, and boots. I don't know much about firearms, but what I saw him carrying was a rifle. A long gun, anyway." She opened her eyes and gave Peller the slightest of smiles. "How did I do?"

"Remarkable," he said with admiration. "But if he was in the woods and dressed to blend in, how could you have seen him that well?"

She shrugged, as though it were nothing. "Practice. The more you look, the easier it becomes to see."

Chapter 9

I have sometimes wondered about the applicability of catastrophe theory to human behavior. A branch of mathematics dealing with phenomena that exhibit sudden shifts in behavior resulting from small changes in conditions— think of a landslide, where the side of a mountain suddenly collapses— catastrophe theory has been used to model aspects of human behavior, both individually and culturally. But I am not an expert in this area, so at most I wonder whether or not a particular situation can be modeled thus.

The temptation was there in the case of the Fibonacci murders. A carefully crafted sequence of events suddenly and without warning gave way to an entirely different sequence of events, just as carefully crafted, on the surface very similar, yet baffling in its differentness. Had something in the killer's mind pushed him over the lip of a cusp and set off a rapid cascade of events that led to the new sequence, as the landslide transforms the very shape of the mountain?

Such speculation may lead to profound insight, but often it is vain imagination. Σ

Monday was Monday all around. Eric Dumas had been helping Captain Morris prepare for her press conference when word of the murdered family came in. Two minutes later, the mathematician arrived looking for Peller. Morris told Dumas to set him up in a cubicle with the files on the murders, after which the detective rushed out to the latest crime scene. Only when he was halfway there did he realize he hadn't thought to ask Tom if he was okay looking at photos of corpses. People unused to such sights could be squeamish. It wouldn't do to bring their precious mathematician in only to frighten him off ten minutes later, but it was too late now to do anything about it.

He arrived at the house abutting the grounds of River Hill High School to find a circus in progress: emergency vehicles, a crowd of anxious and distraught friends and neighbors, and reporting crews of all stripes with recorders and cameras at the ready. He threaded his way through the chaos, trying to look as unofficial as possible until he reached the cordon guarded by five young, grim officers: three men and two women. He flashed his badge and slipped through as a cacophony arose from reporters trying to get his attention.

The house, sporting pale green siding and a two-car garage to the left, proved to be a comfortable upper-middle-class home that had been well-maintained. Inside, the furnishings offered a curious contrast, mostly European assemble-it-yourself stuff in light woods and pastel fabrics. One wall of the living room had been turned into a photo gallery, where pictures of the family—a very extended family, apparently—were proudly displayed.

In the center of the wall hung a large photo of eight people in two rows. In back on the left stood a balding, middle-aged father and at his side his blonde wife, a radiant smile illuminating her face. Beside her, a twentyish man as tall as the father draped an arm around his mother's shoulders and those of a teenage girl whose eyes and smile marked her as his sister. In front, three younger children were arranged boy, girl, boy; while to the right their frail grandmother sat in a low-backed chair, beaming with pride. All were dressed formally: the men and boys in ties and jackets, the women and girls in soft pastel dresses. Although the portrait was posed, there was nothing artificial about the closeness of this family. Dumas thought of Easter and spring weddings.

On the floor beneath the portrait, dressed in the same clothing they had worn for the portrait, eight bodies had been carefully arranged to mimic it. Father, mother, oldest son, and oldest daughter lay on the floor. The other children and grandmother had been placed on top of them. The oldest son's arms had been arranged around his mother's and sister's shoulders; the grandmother bent and slightly turned to suggest a seated posture. Gaping exit wounds shattered their foreheads.

Dumas stood, silent, while the crime scene team swirled around him. Beyond doubt, the lifeless pile of bodies was the worst thing he had ever seen. Monstrous. Heartless. Leo's mocking spirit filled the room.

Officer Graham, who had come from Jamaica so long ago that Dumas couldn't remember a time when he wasn't on the force, came to stand next to Dumas. "What evil thing was here, Eric?" he asked, his accent more marked than usual. "They couldn't possibly have deserved this."

"None of Leo's victims deserved it."

Graham's eyebrows went up. "Leo?"

"Our name for the monster. Long story. Who reported this?"

"A neighbor who came looking for the mother. When there was no answer at the door, she went around back and looked in the window."

"Must've been a terrible shock," Dumas said, and Graham nodded. Dumas turned his attention to the wall to his left. There, a set of eight kitchen chairs had been placed, the easy chairs and table that normally sat there pushed unceremoniously aside to make room. Cut ropes and strips of cloth lay in a heap in front of the chairs. The wall itself was splashed with blood and tissue and gouged where the spent bullets had driven into the sheetrock.

"They were bound and gagged when he killed them," Dumas said.

"Looks like it."

Dumas turned away from the carnage. "Aside from the obvious, what have we got so far, Kevin?"

"We're searching the house and the grounds now. So far nothing seems out of place except..." He cast a quick glance around the room, then looked away.

"Yeah. Damn. I need some air."

Graham pointed to a doorway. "There's a back door out the kitchen."

Dumas made directly for the exit, only noting in passing that the kitchen was pristine: no dirty dishes, no food left lying about, the small table cleared of all items except a vase holding red and yellow artificial flowers. Outside, he leaned heavily against the house and sucked in the cool air. The overcast sky suggested the weatherman had been right in forecasting light rain for the afternoon. A strip of woods separated the back yard from the school grounds beyond. The building and full parking lot were visible through the bare trees.

Earlier in the day, Dumas had been upbeat. Having put a name to the golf club crimes—Julian Szwiec—gave him a sense of accomplishment. It wasn't merely that they were now close to getting a dangerous nutcase off the streets. He felt very deeply that there was a connection between Szwiec and Leo. Sure, proof was lacking, but he couldn't shake the feeling that hiding somewhere in the woodpile of the evidence lay something they'd overlooked that would prove it. Peller needed to see it before he'd believe it and Montufar needed to find a rationale to believe it. Dumas simply felt it, and he trusted his instincts.

But that was this morning. This latest murder had left his emotions shattered. His eyes played over the trees as though searching that metaphorical woodpile.

Trees.

Woods.

Strange, he thought.

Szwiec liked trees. They hid him and gave him cover. That was why he'd chosen Centennial Park. He lived on its edge and used it as a conduit leading him to his victims and safely back home.

And here were the trees again, as they had been in the murders of snowplow driver Mark Patterson and the double murders of Zachary Rymer and Helen Kamber. Granted that trees were never far away in this county, yet it gave Dumas an eerie feeling. As Montufar had predicted, the case seemed to grow more twisted each day.

"Eric?"

With a start, Dumas turned to find Graham at his elbow. "What've we got?"

"Officer Patel found a woman up in the attic."

Dumas blinked. "You mean alive?"

"That's what Patel said. Bound and gagged like the victims, but it doesn't look like she was harmed."

"What the *hell* is this?" he snapped at nobody, then followed Graham back inside. "Where are the EMTs? Go find one. I'll need to talk to the victim if she's in any shape to answer."

"They might all be gone by now, but I'll see what I can do." Graham hurried off.

Dumas returned to the living room. The neatness of the chairs where the family had sat waiting to be killed mocked him. Did they think they were simply the victims of a burglary? When did they begin to suspect that they were marked for death? Who was shot first, who last? What torture their last moments must have been.

No way in hell was this a one-man job. Leo must have had help this time. How else could he tie up eight people without a struggle? The precision of the killing shots was consistent with the previous homicides. But the arrangement of the bodies beneath their photos—that was something new. Something extreme, as though Leo were shouting, "Look at me!"

What was Leo's purpose? He always seemed to have one. He was deliberate. What had been similarly deliberate about the other killings? Dumas recalled all that he could, but since he hadn't worked the cases he didn't have Peller and Montufar's detailed knowledge of them. He couldn't relate the arrangement of the bodies to anything that had gone before.

Nor did he have time to think about it further. A new crime scene officer approached him. "Have you ever seen anything like this?"

Dumas took the proffered bag, astonished by the weapon within. "A Luger? Where did you find it?"

"In a rose bush at the back corner of the house. I had quite a time getting it out without losing my arm. Damned thing has thorns a foot long."

"Must be a rugosa. They're straight out of *Sleeping Beauty.*" Dumas, whose mother had exhibited roses, was fairly knowledgeable about the varieties. Some folks planted rugosas around their homes for security. If that was the case here, it hadn't helped.

He turned the gun over several times, his eyes running over the slanted, reddish grip, the blocky and angular frame, the circular trigger guard, the sleek barrel. He'd seen photos, but never held one in his hand before. What was a World War II pistol doing in his crime scene? Had Leo actually used it? He was too clever to leave behind a murder weapon. The gun must be a distraction—or had some other, more esoteric, meaning to Leo.

He handed the bag back to the officer. "All right. Get this checked for prints and turned over to ballistics as soon as possible."

"Will do."

As the officer walked away, Graham took his place. "The lady from the attic can talk to you now."

Σ

The surgery lasted nearly two hours, after which the surgeon, Dr. Fran Kendrick, came out to talk with the Montufar sisters. She settled them in a comfortable corner where they could have some privacy and told them, "Everything went very well. Eduardo's going to be fine. He'll need some physical therapy and we'll have to monitor his brain functions for awhile, but I don't expect him to have any trouble getting back to normal. He's strong."

Ella gripped Montufar's hand and let out a relieved sigh. Montufar patted her shoulder.

"Eduardo was very lucky," the surgeon continued. "He did receive a concussion, but it doesn't appear to be severe. The fracture is a simple one, so we don't have to worry as much about further injury to the brain tissue. It occurred over the left temporal lobe, which is primarily involved in verbal memory. We'll know more once he's recovered sufficiently to talk with us. The hip fracture was actually more troubling. He's going to be setting off airport metal detectors for the rest of his life, I'm afraid." She flashed Ella an impish grin and got a weak smile in return. "They'll page you once he's awake, and you can see him for just a few minutes. He'll be very groggy and won't feel much like talking. They'll move him up to a room about an hour after that, and you can see him more then. But don't expect too much from him for the rest of today."

Montufar thanked Kendrick and once she was gone leaned heavily against the back of the couch. Ella remained perched on the edge and muttered, "Thank God." She looked back at her sister.

"Once he's recovered," Montufar said, "I'm going to kill him."

Ella laughed. "I'd help you," she said, "but I don't think I'll be up to it."

"I think I can manage it myself." Montufar closed her eyes for a moment and took a few deep breaths. Slowly she became aware of the sounds around her: a couple of older men nearby talking about fishing, a young mother trying to keep a little boy entertained and out of trouble, a voice on the television talking about a homicide in Clarksville.

Her eyes snapped open and focused on the TV in time to see Dumas, twenty feet behind the reporter, climbing into the back of an ambulance. She whipped out her cell phone and called Peller.

Ella glanced at the television and then back at her sister. "What is it?"

"I don't know. I have to check in. Hang on."

Peller answered on the third ring. "How's your brother?" he asked.

"He's recovering from surgery now," she replied. "The doctor says he'll be okay."

"That's a relief."

"What's going on in Clarksville? I just saw the end of a news report. Looks like Eric is on site."

There was a pause while, she suspected, Peller weighed how much to tell her. Finally, he said, "A family of eight was murdered."

"Oh, my God. Children, too?"

"Yes, but you have your own problems right now. We'll give you all the details later. I don't actually know much at the moment. I was at the Harrison murder scene when the call came in. I'm on my way there now to give Eric a hand."

Montufar said nothing. Her first instinct was to get the address and rush over to help. Eduardo probably would have told her to go, but she owed it to him to stay. Besides, couldn't leave Ella alone here.

"I can stop by for a few minutes if you want," Peller offered.

"No, that's okay," she told him. "Help Eric. The two of you nail Leo to the wall." She didn't add, because she didn't want Ella to hear it, *And once you have him hanging there, I'll finish him off.*

Σ

The officer led Dumas outside where an ambulance was parked in the driveway. Looking in, he found a young female EMT tending to a middle-aged, caramel-complexioned woman who looked like she wasn't sure whether to swoon or scream. Either, Dumas thought, would have been appropriate under the circumstances.

"Ms. Chavez?" he asked. Maria Chavez, Graham had informed him, was the cleaning lady. That's all they had learned about her so far.

Wild-eyed, she nodded.

Dumas climbed into the ambulance and perched next to the EMT. "I'm really sorry to have to bother you right now, but it's important. Could I ask you a few questions?"

She nodded again. Dumas hoped she was capable of more.

"Thank you. Can you tell me what happened?"

Another nod, but this time accompanied by a torrent of words in a thick Mexican accent. "I clean every week for Mason family. They are good people. They be nice to me. I am cleaning kitchen when doorbell rings. Two men come in with guns, make everyone sit down and be tied up. The tall man is saying it's not right, too many people. The short man says is easy to fix. He will put me upstairs in a bedroom. But when we get up there he sees the attic door. He laughs at me and pushes me up there. After that I don't know what happens, except I hear lots of shooting." She shuddered. "Lots of shooting. I thought they would come up to shoot me, too. But I hear nothing else until the police come."

So Dumas's guess was right; there had been two of them. On a hunch, he leaned out and called one of the officers over. Tossing him his car keys, he told him to bring the file from the back seat.

"Do you think you could describe these men?" he asked Chavez.

"The tall one, he looks like a soldier. The short one, no. He looks like maybe a computer guy."

Dumas nearly laughed, but he thought he knew what she meant. "The soldier, how tall was he?"

With a shrug, Chavez said, "I don't know. I'm not big, so many people look tall to me."

The officer returned with the requested folder, which contained information on the mad golfer, Julian Szwiec. Dumas pulled out the sketch of Szwiec and held it up before Chavez.

She frowned, but managed to focus on the picture. "Yes. He is the one who locked me in the attic."

Dumas took back the sketch and gazed at it. They had him. Now all they had to do was find him.

"Are you done?" the EMT asked. "We should take Ms. Chavez to the hospital."

"Is she hurt?" Dumas asked, alarmed that he'd forgotten to inquire about that at the outset.

"Nothing serious, but she got knocked around when they shoved her up the stairs. And I'm not really equipped to address the psychological issues. Best to be safe."

Peller arrived moments after the ambulance left. "Looks like I solved your case for you," Dumas told him with a grin, then turned more serious as he filled his colleague in on the details.

"You think Szwiec is Leo, then?" Peller asked.

"Well, maybe. The other man could be Leo. But if Maria Chavez remembered it right, it sounded to me like Szwiec was the one who had the answer to the problem of too many people. That's a Leo-like trait."

"Either way," Peller said, "if we nab one of them we'll have a good chance of nabbing both. I'm going to have a look around. Why don't you call Whitney, give her an update and tell her we need all the lab work on this done yesterday."

"You got it," Dumas said, feeling nearly as upbeat now as he had earlier. It might be cruel to find anything in the situation that might warrant gladness, he reflected, but he was powerless to bring back the dead. What he could do, he hoped, was make sure this family's tragic end was also the end of Leo's career.

Σ

By four forty-five that afternoon, Captain Morris had pushed, pulled, prodded, and intimidated everyone necessary to get the full workup on the latest murders. Most of the results were entirely expected and fairly uninformative, but one thing stood out: a set of clear fingerprints had been lifted from the gun found in the rosebush outside the Mason home. The FBI had promised to run the prints as fast as possible.

Everyone had forgotten about Tom Kaneko, the mathematician, until Peller happened upon him, still sitting in the cubicle Dumas had assigned to him, a pad of notepaper filled with neatly-lettered notes and the case file arranged just so in front of him. He was staring at a crime scene photograph of the double murder victims, Zachary Rymer and Helen Kamber.

"A psychologist may be of more help to you than I can be, Lieutenant Peller," Kaneko said by way of greeting.

"What do you mean?"

Kaneko picked up the photo, still focused on it. "When I first saw the photo of the snowplow driver, I had a flashback to my youth and my first encounter with photos from Hiroshima and Nagasaki. It was quite horrible. But I imagine one grows inured to such sights over time." He turned and handed the photo to Peller. "Doesn't one?"

Peller studied the image. There was nothing new to find. He'd stared a dozen holes through it already over the past couple of days. "I don't know about inured," he told Kaneko. "You focus on what you have to focus on, I guess."

"What do you focus on in this case?"

"Two victims, each killed by a single gunshot to the forehead. The bodies were left as they fell. They must have been standing close together, facing the killer. They knew they were going to die." He set the photo on the desk. He didn't need visual reminders. The scene was so burned into his memory that he was sure it would leave a permanent scar. "Rymer's face is turned towards Kamber, but hers is looking almost straight up. Likely she was killed first."

"One cannot deduce that," Kaneko said. "But it is a reasonable supposition."

Peller tapped the image of Kamber. After the briefest of moments, the mathematician craned forward to look. If Kaneko was disturbed by the photographs, Peller thought, he was, in his own words, becoming inured. "The perpetrator kicked or threw mud on her after killing her."

"Yes. Mud." The mathematician invested the word with a gravity that chilled Peller. "That is what drew most my attention. This is the act of one who despises his victim, or wishes to degrade her. Do you believe the murderer hated this young woman?"

"Probably not. There's reason to think he had watched the couple in order to understand their movements, but we have no reason to think he knew either of them. There's nothing to suggest that Leo knew any of his victims."

Kaneko cocked his head. Peller thought he looked like a dog whose curiosity had been piqued. "So why commit an act of hatred? Curious, isn't?"

Peller picked up the photo again, a frown fixed on his lips. "Very. What are you suggesting?"

"Leo made some connection between Helen Kamber, who he never knew, and someone who he knows and despises." He turned to the file on the desk and extracted the photograph of Mark Patterson, the snowplow driver. "You won't see the crucial fact about this murder in the photograph."

Peller took the photo, glanced at it, then set it back on the desk. Again, he didn't need to see it to know what it showed. "What would that be?" he asked, curious what the mathematician would suggest.

Kaneko placed both photographs back in the file. "The killer was waiting to kill someone in particular."

"I doubt that. We've tried without success to connect Patterson with anything that might have marked him for death. He appears to simply have been in the wrong place at the wrong time."

As if reading Peller's thoughts, Kaneko allowed a slight smile and continued, "I don't mean he was waiting for Mr. Patterson personally. But consider: if you are going to kill someone driving down a primary street, and you choose to commit the murder during or after a heavy snowfall, who are you guaranteed to find if you but wait a short while?"

"A snowplow driver," Peller said. "We've considered that. But we can't get past one problem. What's the point of killing a snowplow driver? It's a dicey way to start a series of murders. How do you know you'll get the snowstorm?"

"Snowstorms aren't that uncommon here. At most Leo might have had to postpone his plans until next year."

Peller couldn't help but laugh. "That degree of patience would be creepy."

"Which Leo is," Kaneko said, not laughing.

Peller had to admit that. "Granted. But what's the point of killing a snowplow driver? Why do you say that's the key detail?"

"These are not random acts. The Fibonacci sequence is very specific. As with Ms. Kamber, Leo made a connection between a snowplow driver he never knew and someone he did know."

"You mean someone who drives a snowplow?"

Kaneko shook his head. "Not necessarily, but someone who drives something big, something that may in some ways be like a snowplow."

Peller sat on the edge of the desk and looked from Kaneko to the photos. "You're saying these are reenactments of events Leo experienced earlier." It made as much sense as anything else they'd considered, but even if Kaneko was right, it didn't seem to put them much closer to stopping Leo. He could be reenacting almost anything. "You think the other murders fit that pattern?"

"Exactly. Each murder," Kaneko said in a tone reminiscent of a professor concluding a proof on a whiteboard and setting down the marker, "contains such a deliberate feature, different each time, quite subtle, and almost certainly of great significance to the killer."

Chapter 10

At the end of a logical proof it is customary to write "Q.E.D.," the acronym for "quod erat demonstrandum," the Latin for "which was to be demonstrated." It is a signal that the proof has been successfully concluded. None of us realized at the time that the execution of the Mason family marked the end of a proof of sorts. The killer had concluded a demonstration that was to have a more chilling consequence still. But it had not been stamped "Q.E.D.," so the fact only became clear in hindsight. Σ

Once out of recovery, Eduardo drifted in and out of sleep for the rest of the day. He managed a few smiles along the way, sufficient to reassure his sisters that it was okay to go home and get some sleep themselves. Ella had regained sufficient optimism to do so, but Montufar found sleep difficult. Though the details of the Mason killings trickled out with successive news updates throughout the day, she knew that her colleagues had much more information than the reporters. She had the feeling that whatever it was that had so far eluded her about Leo would become clear if she could only get that information.

By the time Tuesday morning dawned, she'd had quite enough of on-again, off-again sleep. She dressed and drove to headquarters, grabbing a fast food breakfast along the way and arriving well before her colleagues. Pulling up the computer files on the latest murders, she pored over them, forcing herself to remain detached.

Once she had absorbed everything, she went to the break room for a cup of coffee then, spilling not a drop of the steaming liquid, rushed back to her desk where she ticked off items on a mental checklist. Mark Patterson, sniper attack. Andrew Carrington, shot point-blank in a corridor. Zachary Rymer and Helen Kamber, surprised and shot in the woods. Lorna Bigelow, killed surreptitiously in her sleep, the only victim who hadn't been shot. Roger Harrison, another sniper attack. The Masons, lined up and executed in their own home.

A chill ran down Montufar's spine. She laid her head on her desk and folded her hands over it as if curling into a defensive posture, or hiding from the world.

She knew what it was.

God in heaven, she knew what it was.

$$\Sigma$$

By the time Peller and Dumas arrived, headquarters was a hive of activity. In addition to the usual cases, six crank calls claiming responsibility for the previous day's killings had come in, while eight letters from would-be mad golfers and serial killers had been delivered. Captain Morris had intended to release Julian Szwiec's name and particulars and ask the public for information on his whereabouts, but the Mason killings had preempted everything, so now she was in overdrive, attempting to gather information for the rescheduled press conference to cover both Szwiec and the hunt for Leo. The fact that Szwiec was implicated in the Mason killings was, from her view, a strong positive development. The fact that he'd slipped through their fingers the day before, however, was going to make things very ugly.

Tom Kaneko had returned to his borrowed cubicle and was busy reviewing the latest information, his concentration so intense he didn't notice the bedlam surrounding him.

And then there was Montufar, looking pale and exhausted as she hooked both Peller and Dumas by the arm and steered them towards an empty conference room. "We have to talk," she said.

"How's your brother?" they asked simultaneously.

"He'll live," she replied. "We have a bigger problem."

She pushed them into the conference room and was about the close the door when a voice cried from across the room, "Phone call, Lieutenant." Peller craned his neck to look around Montufar. A new detective whose name he couldn't recall pointed emphatically at the receiver he was holding aloft and mouthed what looked like, "It's him."

"Transfer it in here," Peller called back. When the phone rang he pushed the speaker button. "Peller," he spat.

"Hello again, my friend," Leo's thin voice murmured.

"I'm not your friend," the detective growled.

A rattling laugh sounded on the other end. "But I will do you a favor anyway. Some new information. Write this down."

Dumas pulled a pen and notepad from his pocket and nodded.

"Go ahead," Peller said.

"I start with two."

They all stared at the phone, even Dumas, who wrote nothing.

"What?" Peller demanded.

"I start with two," Leo repeated. There was a click and the line went dead.

Dumas looked confused. "Didn't we already start with zero?" he asked, but scribbled down the message anyway.

Montufar pulled out a chair and collapsed into it, shutting her eyes.

Peller dialed an extension and told the person on the other end, "Have Tom join us in the conference room, please." Sinking into a chair next to Montufar, he asked her, "What did you want to talk to us about?" The calmness in his voice amazed even himself.

She opened her eyes. "I think he's a soldier. Or used to be one."

Dumas nodded. "I can see that. Or possibly a cop gone bad. That would account for the haircut. And it's clear he knows his way around firearms. A Luger? That's not your average gun."

"It's more than that," Montufar continued. "It's the way each killing has been planned and executed. A couple of sniper attacks, a couple of executions. One like an encounter in a narrow street, except it was a service corridor in the mall, and even one—Lorna Bigelow—that might be like a covert assassination. I think this guy was in Iraq or Afghanistan and brought the war home with him."

Peller let the idea chase its tail around his brain until Dumas interrupted: "Problem."

They waited while he formulated his thoughts. "Look at it this way," he began, but got no further as Kaneko abruptly opened the door.

"You wanted to see me?" the mathematician asked.

Peller motioned him to a chair. "Leo called again."

Kaneko sat. "I thought he said eight was the last number?" Dumas shoved the notepad to him, and he gazed at it without expression.

"What do you think?" Peller asked.

"I think we are in trouble. What do you think?"

Peller sighed heavily. "He's starting a new sequence."

Dumas added, "It starts the same way as the first sequence. 'I start with...' The numbers in the new sequence will have the same meanings as the ones in the first sequence."

Kaneko nodded, "Likely so. But we will need at least three numbers before we have a chance of determining what this new sequence is."

"I'd think," Peller said, "it would be obvious. If it follows the Fibonacci pattern, it would be two, three, five, eight, thirteen, twenty-one, and thirty-four."

There was a moment of silence that seemed to drag on and on. Then Kaneko stood and began to walk slowly around the table, hands clasped behind his back. "What troubles me in this particular situation," he began, "is that the Fibonacci sequence, which you are familiar with, is merely a special case of something called a Lucas sequence, which you most likely do *not* know. Technically, a complementary pair of Lucas sequences generate the Fibonacci sequence. A Lucas sequence is specified by a recurrence relation and a pair of fixed integers. So there are an infinite number of such sequences and thus an infinite number of complementary pairs of such sequences. And Lucas sequences are merely one type of sequence. It is impossible to know what sequence one is dealing with if all one has is a single number. Indeed, it is impossible to know based on two consecutive numbers."

"Clear as mud," Dumas said with the petulant air of one whose academic strengths did not include mathematics.

"Um, okay," Montufar said, taking up the slack. "You're right, none of us know about Lucas sequences. We didn't know about Fibonacci until this all started. But what does it mean, that he's using a Lucas sequence? I know what an integer is, but what makes them fixed? What's a recurrence relation? How can we use it to help predict the next murder, and how likely is it that Leo knows it?"

Kaneko stopped pacing and gazed at his shoes. "Not likely," he admitted. "Yet I suggest that we reserve judgment."

"Point taken," Peller said. "Thank you."

Kaneko bowed slightly and withdrew.

"So what we're looking at," said Dumas to Peller, "is a psychopathic soldier who was a mathematician in a past life and who just happens to know you even though you don't know him? Are we actually getting anywhere with this?" He took back his notepad and studied what he'd written. "What if… " he mused, "what if…despite higher mathematics…Leo isn't just a psycho? What if he doesn't think he's still fighting the war? What if he thinks he's fighting *a* war, though, and he's told us more or less how he's going to fight it? Up to now he's been saying, 'This is what I'm going to do.' But now—" he pushed the notepad to Peller—"now he's saying, 'I'm going to start doing it.' He either wants us to stop him before he does it, or he wants the world to know that he's the one doing it."

None of them had noticed that Captain Morris had quietly opened the door and was listening until she rapped on the wall. "Sorry to interrupt," she said, "but I want the three of you with me at the press conference to answer any questions I can't answer. And I want us to agree on one thing before we get there. Job one is nabbing Julian Szwiec. All speculation aside, if he was at the Mason home, then he can lead us to his partner and that's the end of it."

Peller didn't think it would be that easy, but it wasn't the time to argue. Without a word, he nodded assent, and the three of them rose to follow their boss.

Σ

Every TV station and newspaper in the Mid-Atlantic region plus CNN and the BBC seemed to have jammed journalists into the lobby of Northern District Headquarters, where Captain Morris had instructed a lectern and a small table and several chairs to be placed for the press conference. The cacophony, she thought, could drown out the most over-amped rock concert ever played at Merriweather Post Pavilion. Yet when she came into the gathering followed by Peller, Montufar, and Dumas, a sudden silence descended. The detectives took seats at the table while she marched straight to the lectern and began quickly, so as not to allow anyone else time to get in a word.

"Good morning. For those of you who don't know, I'm Captain Whitney Morris, head of the Howard County Police Criminal Investigations Division. With me are Detective Lieutenant Rick Peller, Detective Sergeant Corina Montufar, and Detective Sergeant Eric Dumas. We're here today with updates on the so-called golfer muggings and the series of murders that have taken place in Howard County over the past week. I know you're anxious to get to the latter, but first I want to give you some information about the muggings."

Some muttering erupted in the crowd, but Morris paid it no heed. "Previously we released a sketch of a suspect. Thanks to information provided by a witness who saw that sketch on the news, we have been able to identify the suspect as Julian Szwiec, age twenty-two, currently unemployed. Mr. Szwiec is armed and dangerous. During a pursuit he shot and wounded two officers who discovered him at his home near Centennial Park in Columbia. Anyone having any information about Mr. Szwiec's whereabouts should immediately contact our department. Do not attempt to approach or apprehend him yourself. Again, he is armed and extremely dangerous."

She paused for a look around the room. So far she sensed she was delivering what they wanted to hear, but that wasn't going to last long. "There is one more thing," she told them. "As you know, not one but two terrible tragedies occurred yesterday: the brutal murders of an entire family in Clarksville, and the murder of state senator Roger Harrison. Both of these murders appear to be related to the killings committed over the past week. But the murders of the Mason family, as tragic as they were, may have given us the means to put a stop to these horrible acts and bring the guilty parties to justice. We have strong evidence that Julian Szwiec was present in the Mason home that morning along with another man."

Pandemonium erupted. Every reporter in the room shouted out questions and gestured wildly in a frantic bid for attention. Morris called for quiet several times but could barely hear herself over the din. Finally, she stepped back from the microphone and put her hands on her hips, directing a motherly scowl at the throng. Oddly enough, the noise gradually died down. She stepped forward and continued.

"I know you all have questions," she told them, "and we're here to answer them as best we can. But first let me give you the details as we know them."

For the next five minutes Morris laid out the basic information on the shooting of Roger Harrison, including the description of the killer as given to Peller by Virginia Smullyan, and a somewhat less detailed account of the Mason family murders. She left out the news that a gun had been located and said only that an eyewitness had put Szwiec at the scene at about the time of the killings. She did call the killings "execution-style," which prompted another outburst of raised hands and questions.

The first question Morris took was the one she had been dreading. The *Bal-*

timore Sun reporter asked trenchantly, "So your officers let Julian Szwiec escape, after which he killed the Masons?"

"Mr. Szwiec was armed and fled into the woods of Centennial Park when the two officers tried to apprehend him. He shot them in the ensuing chase, after which they were unable to continue the pursuit. We do not know yet whether he killed the Masons. We do know that he was there and that he played some role in the crime, but there was one other person with him, who might be the real killer. Either way, we view the apprehension of Mr. Szwiec as instrumental in ending this killing spree."

Morris signaled the CNN reporter, a pixieish redhead with a scattering of freckles across her nose. "Do you have any evidence that Szwiec was involved in the other killings?"

"Not at this time," Morris replied.

Before the Captain could call on someone else, the reporter fired off another question. "So was he *at* the Mason home or *in* the Mason home? And if he was *in* the Mason home, how would you know that?"

"I'll let Detective Dumas answer that question." Morris cast a sidelong glance at her colleague.

Dumas pulled the table microphone over. "He was in the house. We have a witness who places him there at the time of the murders."

Morris gave him a small, quick smile. *Nice deflection,* she thought.

Except the reporter wasn't deflected. "So there was someone in the house who *wasn't* killed?"

Dumas assumed a poker face. "There are many ways a witness might place someone inside a house at a particular time, ma'am. With the killer still at large, we don't want to reveal too much about that so as not to endanger the witness."

Morris almost laughed. The man had a definite theatrical streak. She signaled the NPR reporter.

"You said previously that these killings are related to Fibonacci numbers. Do yesterday's murders follow that pattern and can you elaborate on what exactly it is?"

"They do follow that pattern," Morris said. "But that's all I can say at this moment."

"Well, if the murders are each linked to successive numbers in the sequence," the journalist pointed out, "anyone can see that the next few numbers are very large.

Are we talking about body counts? Are we looking at something like a terrorist attack?"

Before Morris could reply, Peller took the microphone. "These are not terrorist attacks," he said sharply. "People are right to be concerned, but we have no immediate reason to fear another 9/11. The numbers are related to the murders in a complicated way that we are not at liberty to discuss."

Morris next selected a cub reporter for the local newspaper, *The Columbia Flier*. He had a somewhat timid look about him, as though he wasn't sure he should be speaking at all. She hoped that meant his question would be easy.

"I wanted to ask Sergeant Montufar—" he began, and the detectives exchanged surprised glances—"how is your brother doing?"

Montufar didn't know the young man from Adam, and the question crept up her spine. Hesitantly, she took the microphone. "He's doing okay," she said. "Why do you ask?"

"Well..." The reporter glanced around at his colleagues a bit sheepishly. "I sort of know your sister Ella. She mentioned the accident but didn't have time to go into details."

Montufar took a relieved breath and smiled at him. "I don't think she's mentioned you before." That got a general laugh, and the young man's face flushed scarlet. "But thank you. He's doing fine."

Chapter 11

It had occurred to me, if not to the police, that in the age of the Internet it was not necessary to be highly trained in mathematics to make use of relatively complex mathematical concepts. I don't mean that just anyone might learn to calculate third order differential equations by reading a website, but most any reasonably intelligent person could, with sufficient effort, teach themselves how to calculate various forms of sequences.

This led me to a conclusion I did not at once share with Rick Peller. That failure to consult was a mistake. Σ

Until the new sequence began to take shape, Tomio Kaneko didn't see much he could do to help the detectives, and in any case he had classes to teach on Tuesday afternoon. So he left headquarters shortly before noon and returned to his home in the well-heeled Baltimore neighborhood just north of the Johns Hopkins University campus. His house, set amid early twentieth-century homes—some of which bordered on mansions—was one of the more modest in the area. Kaneko disliked pretense and ostentation, but he and his wife Sarah had raised six children, so living space was a necessity. And now that they had three grandchildren, with one more on the way, he couldn't see downsizing.

He pulled into the left bay of his three-car garage and pushed the button on the remote to close the door. Once inside he made his way to the kitchen, where he found Sarah heating up a pot of soup and assembling a couple of chicken salad sandwiches. She flashed him a radiant smile. "I knew you'd be home for lunch," she said, "so I thought I'd throw something together."

He put a hand on her shoulder and squeezed gently. Her smile hadn't changed in forty years. He remembered little of the day they met except for her smile. She was a thin woman, about the same height as himself, with short, dark hair. She had Japanese ancestry like himself, but also Portuguese heritage on her mother's side. It was hard to say whether her features should be classified as Asian or European.

"Have you been able to help them?" she asked.

He sat at the table and watched her work. "It is hard to know. I have studied all the material they could give me, but there is little to go on in terms of the mathematical angle of the case. I am very much afraid more people will die before I can tell them anything useful."

She must have detected a note of frustration or sadness in his voice, he thought, because she stopped what she was doing and turned to face him with a resolute expression. "You are not a policeman. They probably knew it was a long shot asking you to help them."

"Yes. Still, I wish I could do more. And perhaps I can."

Sarah didn't ask. She brought the meal to the table and sat next to him. They ate in silence for a time while he mulled over whether or not to tell her what he had in mind. Sarah had always been supportive, even when his ideas were slightly harebrained. Not that he had ever been much of a maverick, although he did sometimes have his moments. But this was likely more harebrained than anything he'd previously done.

"It occurs to me," he finally said, "that this killer might once have been a student with some talent for mathematics. He seems quite methodical. The police believe he was overseas in the military. So perhaps he is a young man who returned from his tour of duty with mental problems."

She lifted a spoonful of soup to her lips and blew on it, then made a show of slurping it up. Kaneko had to laugh in spite of himself. Having gotten his attention, she repeated, "You are not the police."

"But if I can help…"

"You might get into trouble."

"I don't think so. All I intend to do is make some inquiries of colleagues and draw up a list of possible suspects. I will then turn that over to Detective Peller."

She gave him a skeptical look.

He shrugged.

"I know you, Tomio. You won't be satisfied with a long list of possible suspects. You are driven to find solutions. You'll try to winnow it down, and that will mean making contact with at least some of the people on the list."

Kaneko studied his hands for a moment. "Yes. I suppose it will. But I can't sit by and do nothing while people are dying."

"People are always dying. I had family there, too. In both Hiroshima and Nagasaki. Now we have family here, our children and our grandchildren and, God willing, many more generations to come. We must serve the present and the future, not the past."

He looked her in the eyes. She wasn't afraid. She was just talking sense as she saw it. But so was he. "I agree," he told her. "And that is why I must do this."

Sarah studied his face for a few moments. "Then I will help."

$$\Sigma$$

Jerry Souter caught the press conference entirely by accident. One of the Baltimore news/talk stations had carried it live, and he just happened to have his radio on at the time because the quiet of his house had started to drive him nuts. Once upon a time his wife Amanda and three kids had kept the place in fairly perpetual chaos, but the children were grown and after Amanda's death from cancer they didn't come around very often. She had been the one who held the family together, not him.

Not that he much complained about their absence, but the quiet, that was something else again. He didn't think he'd ever get used to it. The radio sometimes helped, although he didn't care for the music played by most stations these days. He didn't care for talk radio as such, either, but he was pretty good at tuning out the actual words and allowing the chatter of voices to form a backdrop to his day.

The press conference, though, that was personal. He knew and liked Peller, and was interested in hearing what the police had to say about the crimes. Once it was over, he thought he might walk down to the deli three blocks away and grab a bite to eat. The weather was cool, around fifty degrees, but the sky was mostly clear and the wind light, so he pulled on a light coat and made his way carefully down the steps from his porch to the walk. *One of these days,* he thought, *I should put a ramp in. But not out front. Maybe in back. Don't want people to think to think I'm old.*

He took a casual look around as he approached the sidewalk along the street. This time of day the neighborhood tended to be quiet, with only light traffic, most adults away at work, the children off to school. So it wasn't difficult to notice the young man standing across the street two doors down. He was wrapped in an overcoat and his eyes were nearly covered with the rim of a floppy brown hat. The guy looked like he was trying real hard not to look like a spy, Souter thought, which probably meant he was up to no good.

Souter walked a dozen steps in the other direction, toward the deli, then stopped and turned quickly. The other man had been approaching him at a rapid clip, but once discovered pretended to drop something and lean over to pick it up.

"I'm on to you," Souter called out, then continued on his way, listening for the sound of approaching footfalls but hearing nothing.

At the deli he bought a chicken, cheese, and tomato sandwich and a glass of iced tea. Business was slow, so he chatted with the owner while he ate, discussing the upcoming baseball season and the slim prospects for the Orioles to pull out of their long slump. Afterwards, he made his way back to his house.

While still a block away, he saw that the man in the trench coat was still there, shuffling his feet as though waiting interminably for a bus and, it appeared, keeping a close eye on Peller's house.

Souter made a nonchalant turn onto a cross street and walked just far enough to be out of the man's view. Then he pulled his cell phone from his left trouser pocket and called Peller.

Σ

"A young man in a trench coat, watching your house," Dumas said very deliberately after Peller told him what Souter had reported. "Now I wonder who that could be."

Peller tossed the wrappings of his fast-food lunch into the break room trash can. "It doesn't make much sense, though. Why would Szwiec stake out my place in broad daylight? And why would he threaten a passerby while doing so?"

They both looked to Montufar, who was busy washing up a plastic container. "Don't ask me," she said. "It's a nutty situation. You're the one with all the nutty ideas, Eric. This should be right up your alley."

He laughed, knowing she'd meant it as a backhanded compliment. "Well. Maybe he's just stupid."

"In which case he's not Leo," Peller said. "I'll get an unmarked car sent over there to pick him up. This is almost too easy."

Dumas frowned. "Hell. It is, isn't it?"

Before he could explain, Peller's cell phone sounded Captain Morris's ring tone. "What's up?" Peller asked her.

"Another double murder, a couple of teenagers found dead in a picnic shelter at the west end of Patuxent River State Park. You also got another letter."

"From Leo?" Peller asked, stunned.

"Seems so. He must have managed to hand-deliver it. No postage, no return address, just your name on the envelope. Inside it says..." Paper rattled for a moment. Peller took the opportunity to put his phone on speaker so the others could hear. "It says, 'Killed with three shots, for once deservedly so.'"

The break room went silent. Then Dumas said, "Corina wanted a nutty idea, so here it is. Leo's going to get rid of Sczweic, and he's going to do it right on Rick's doorstep."

"*What?*" Morris said.

Peller filled her in on the call from Jerry Souter. "Get some officers over there fast. If nothing's happening on the street, they have my permission to break down my door and see what's inside. Corina and I will take the park murders. Eric, you head over to my place in case we're too late. Which we probably are."

Dumas spun around and sprinted out of the building to his car. As he tore out of the parking lot, tires squealing, he mentally flogged himself for being so blind. In hindsight the two cases, so different at the outset, had been on a collision course all along. Leo had hinted at the connection when he spattered mud on Helen Kamber's body and left her ring lying nearby. When he involved Julian Szwiec in the slaughter of the Mason family, he had sealed his accomplice's fate. The gun found in the rosebush, Dumas knew, would have Szwiec's fingerprints on it, not Leo's. No matter who actually pulled the trigger, the evidence would point only to Szwiec. And now Szwiec had been set up for death on Peller's doorstep.

Weaving in and out of traffic while horns honked and drivers cursed, Dumas approached Peller's neighborhood from the west while keeping tabs on radio reports from officers in the three unmarked cars converging on the area and the four squads quietly moving into position to close off possible escape routes. He was still three blocks away when the chatter picked up:

"Is that him? Must be. Caucasian male wearing an overcoat and a big hat. Looks like he's right at the edge of Peller's property."

"Okay, we're at the south end of the block, just around the corner."

"You see him?"

"Yeah."

"Okay, both ends of the block are covered."

"Car 27 in position."

"Car 14 in position."

"Tyler, you guys back us up. We'll drive in and try to take him quietly."

Dumas stopped on the cross street half a block behind the unmarked car at the west end of the block and announced his presence, then got out of the car and walked casually forward until he could take in the action. He found Szwiec there, shuffling along in front of Peller's house as if lost. But he must have been wary of the approaching vehicle, for as it came to a stop next to him he turned on his heels and fled. Officers sprang from their cars, guns drawn. Someone shouted, "Police! Stop!" From the other end of the street, more policemen appeared in front of Szwiec, who darted into a driveway. For a few moments Dumas couldn't see anything, but he drew his own weapon and moved cautiously into the yard of the house nearest him. If Szwiec doubled back, he might be able to make his way through the back yards and come out here.

Shouted orders echoed among the houses, drawing closer. Dumas found himself in a fenced-in back yard, chain link on three sides but blocked by a six-foot privacy fence in the next yard over. He was about to return to the front when a terrified face appeared above the fence. Szwiec had tried to scale it but only got far enough to see Dumas. He hung there for a moment, then dropped out of sight as Dumas called out, "Stop! Don't move!"

A gunshot sounded. One of the fence pickets exploded in a shower of splinters and something whistled by the detective's right ear. He threw himself to the ground, training his gun on the fence, but had no way of knowing where Szwiec might be.

"That way!" one of the officers yelled. "That way! He's out front again!"

From the direction of the street, three more shots sounded. Dumas picked himself up and, maintaining as much cover as possible, made his way to the front yard. When he got there, he saw Szwiec lying face-down in the middle of the road as the officers converged on him, weapons at the ready. A squad car had moved in to block each end of the street.

A handful of curious neighbors emerged from their houses. "Get inside!" Dumas shouted, trying to turn every direction at once. "Everybody get inside!" But Szwiec wasn't moving, and in spite of the danger, the gawkers remained.

Dumas approached the officers, who were talking in hushed tones. "Suspect down," one of them was saying into the microphone clipped to his lapel. "We need an ambulance."

"Who shot him?" another asked.

"Wasn't me."

Heads shook and more denials were muttered.

The first speaker exploded, "Damn it, one of us had to have done it!" He looked pointedly at Dumas.

"I didn't fire a shot," he said, "although I almost caught one myself back there."

An ambulance siren sounded in the distance, growing closer. One of the officers knelt to examine the suspect. "Guy's dead," he reported. "He's not breathing."

Dumas bent over Szwiec's body and scrutinized it from various angles. "Head shots," he said, pointing at the left side of the head. "Entrance wounds here and here and here. Three of them." He felt his stomach do a backflip. "Damn it!" He straightened and glared at each of the nearby houses in turn as though willing them to explode.

"What?" one of the officers asked.

"Get a crime scene unit out here right away," Dumas ordered. "And make sure nobody leaves this neighborhood until we've canvassed all the houses. None of us killed him. He was murdered. Right in front of us, he was murdered!"

Σ

After lunch, Kaneko sent emails to fifteen colleagues in the Washington/Baltimore area inquiring after students who showed an aptitude for mathematics and who were known to have either left their studies to join the military or to have joined the military after graduation. It had taken him some time to figure out how to phrase the request without raising suspicion. By the time he was talking with Sarah about it, he'd settled on a blatant lie, but one that he thought could be justified by the circumstances: he presented himself as looking into the feasibility of a study on the contribution of university mathematics departments to the military and hinted that such a study could provide support for government grant proposals in the future. To be most effective, he said, the study would need to look not just at students graduating from mathematics programs but also those who simply had gained a solid mathematical background regardless of their courses of study or, indeed, if they had even earned a degree.

Responses were not long in coming. By afternoon Kaneko had heard back from over half of his contacts, some offering names of former students and some offering suggestions regarding the design of the study. He found the latter amusing if not unexpected, since the study was a ruse.

The names, however, were of interest. Most, it seemed, had been majoring in science or technical arenas. A few had graduated before joining the military, but most had not. In some cases economic factors were mentioned, while a few students had apparently felt the call of duty. For most part, however, their math professors only knew that they were gone.

But that didn't matter. The question Kaneko cared most about was not why they had gone, but which ones were now back home.

Chapter 12

Strictly speaking, causality is the realm of philosophers, not mathematicians. Yet causal relationships are relationships, and certain aspects of relationships do fall into the realm of mathematics. Consider the case of Julian Szwiec. Although seemingly uninvolved in the killings at first, as events unfolded the fact, if not the nature, of his relationship to them became obvious. Ultimately he became one of the victims.

While the police pursued information as to his background, I saw something clearly: Szwiec and the killer were elements of distinct intersecting sets. The parameters defining those sets could reveal the nature of the intersection and lead to identification of the killer. $\sum$

At the west end of Patuxent River State Park, a twelve-mile-long stretch of forested land snaking along the Patuxent River, an access road dotted with picnic shelters had become the latest focal point in Leo's killing spree. Word of the discovery of two more bodies had leaked out, and the news crews arrived just behind Peller and Montufar. Fortunately the shelter where the murders had occurred was a good third of a mile into the park. With the road cordoned off, the crime scene unit was able to work undisturbed.

The officers guarding the crime scene passed them through. Peller was glad to see that one of the investigators was Kevin Graham. "What have we got here, Kevin?" he asked.

Graham's voice was a mixture of soberness, sadness, and disgust. "Sheila Cavenaugh and Ronice Sheppard. Both seventeen. Three weeks till Sheppard's birthday, according to her driver's license. Looks like they were cutting class and doing drugs when Leo caught up with them. Sheppard brought the pot and Cavenaugh had the cocaine. We bagged the stuff they were carrying."

Cavenaugh was a brunette with fair skin, Sheppard a rather shorter black girl. Both were dressed in tattered jeans, pullover sweaters, and light jackets; both had the painful thinness of a habitual drug user. Both had been shot in the back of the head.

"Looks like a sneak attack," Peller said. "They probably never even knew he was there."

Two more half-burned joints lay on the concrete pad near the bodies in positions suggesting that the victims had been smoking when they were shot. "Toxicology can tell us more about what they were on," Graham said. "It's a bad business. They're just kids, even if they're messed up. Are you any closer to catching old Leo?"

Peller shook his head. "I wish I could tell you something different."

"Well," said Graham, the island ringing in his voice, "fight the good fight. Carry on, mon." And with that farewell, he turned back to his crime scene.

Montufar surveyed the bodies sadly. "It's bad enough having to tell people their child is dead without having to tell them that she's on drugs, too."

"Maybe that's who they learned it from," Peller observed cynically. When Montufar made a distressed sound, he apologized. "Sorry. This case is starting to get to me. Insult to injury," he agreed in a subdued voice. "I can only imagine what my parents would say in a similar situation. But I'm old, Corina. I remember the days before cell phones and Reddit." He circled the scene. "They fell face-forward, so they were likely shot from over that way." He pointed westward towards a thick stand of woods, then made his way towards the trees, scanning the ground as he went.

Montufar took a deep breath, letting the cool air fill her lungs. A faint scent of pine carried in on the light breeze to blow away any lingering stink of cannabis and blood. She suddenly felt a piercing longing to be elsewhere—a sunny mountainside, the shore of an ice-kissed lake, the chapel of an alpine monastery—some place where she could once again find purity. The filth of this case seemed to have taken an obscene life and burrowed into her pores, sinking claws deep into her soul. For the first time since she took up a law enforcement career, she wondered if she had chosen the right path.

Peller returned. "I think he was back there," he told her, "but it's hard to tell. We'll look, but I doubt we'll find anything. Those two were like all the rest. Victims of opportunity. But how did Leo know he would find them here? He needed two victims. Somehow he must have known they would be here. Did he know them? Was he watching them?"

Montufar gazed across the road, the opposite direction from which the shots had apparently come. "That last message," she said. "'For once deservedly so.' He's been killing people who he didn't think deserved to die. Why would he do that?"

Peller shook his head.

"He has to be going somewhere with all of this. It can't just be a string of random victims knocked off based on a sequence of numbers picked from a hat."

Peller's cell phone went off. "Why not?" he asked. "Maybe Leo really is just a psycho."

"But…"

"What's up, Eric?" he said into the phone.

Montufar waited while Peller listened. A few heavy-looking clouds moved in from the northwest.

"You're kidding." He rubbed the back of his head. He could feel the tension headache already building. "All right. At least the citizens of the county are safe from golf clubs. We didn't get much here, big surprise. Let's meet back at HQ as soon as possible to pull all the details together. Better get Kaneko to come in, too, so we can fill him in."

Montufar watched him slip the phone back into its holder. "Szwiec's dead?"

"Shot three times in the head while our guys were chasing him down. Deservedly so, as the man said."

"Wait a minute. It was supposed to look like *we* shot him?"

"Maybe."

"Is Leo getting clumsy? A gun tossed aside, presumably to implicate Szwiec, after which Szwiec is murdered during a police chase? Or is this supposed to be murder by cop?"

Peller shrugged and stared at nothing.

"Geez, maybe you're right," she said. "Maybe he is just a psycho."

Σ

Even with Captain Morris pushing and pulling nonstop, it was nearly eight o'clock before reports, photographs, detectives, and a mathematician were assembled in one conference room. Pizzas had been delivered and were half consumed, boxes and soda cans cluttering one end of the table, when the medical examiner's report showed up in Morris's inbox and she printed it out. It contained no surprises. Szwiec had died from severe brain trauma resulting from three gunshot wounds to the head. The evidence suggested that the shots had been fired from a distance and above the victim, probably from an upper-story window in a nearby house.

"If he was there, though," Dumas said, "he must have gotten in and out pretty quietly. Nobody who was home was aware of anyone in their house, and there was no evidence that any of the houses had been broken into. By the way, Rick, we owe you a new window. You said it was okay."

Peller reached for another slice of pepperoni pizza. "I take it you didn't find anything there, either."

"Not a thing."

Montufar was shuffling through printed copies of reports. "I don't get it."

Morris leaned back and gave a nervous laugh. "I don't get any of this!"

Montufar took no notice. "The gun at the Mason home has Szwiec's fingerprints all over it, but nobody else's. Everything we know about Leo tells us he wouldn't do that. So obviously we're supposed to think that Szwiec killed the Masons and tossed the gun. But why would Leo think we'd be fooled by such an obvious trick? People who are disposing of murder weapons don't just throw them into rose bushes, no matter how thorny. They throw them in the river, or drop them in the harbor, or bury them in garbage and haul them to the dump. Shouldn't this occur to Leo?""

His head cradled in his hands, Dumas said, "It should."

"Exactly. So why was the gun tossed?"

The question hung in the air, unanswerable.

"Now," she went on, "Leo sets up Szwiec. The cops move in to arrest him, he bolts, and in the middle of the chase Leo kills him. Again, the obvious conclusion is that we're supposed to think one of the cops shot him."

Peller tapped another report. "Which is impossible. It says here the wounds are more consistent with a sniper rifle than a police weapon. Besides, Leo already told us the magic number: three shots."

"Unless," Dumas added, "we suddenly have another killing with three shots." Absently, he fished in his pants pocket and retrieved a half dollar which he tossed from hand to hand while thinking.

Kaneko, who had been silent for a long time, spoke up: "We don't understand the new sequence yet. Three could indeed be the next number. However, the meaning of the numbers was established by the initial sequence, so it would not be three shots. It would be a third child, probably a son."

"I meant it might be a ruse," Dumas said.

Kaneko shook his head. "Leo is methodical. He will not break the sequence. He must kill five more times to fulfill the pattern set up by the first sequence, and each position in this sequence must have the same meaning as in the first sequence."

"And that's the problem," Montufar said. "Why go to the trouble of implicating Szwiec in the Mason killings and then the cops in the killing of Szwiec if it's painfully obvious that Leo was the killer both times?"

Dumas palmed the coin, then stared at his apparently relaxed hand. The others nodded approval, unable to tell that he was hiding Kennedy. "He staged it all."

"We know that," Peller said. "But why?"

"I don't mean he staged it for our benefit, to fool us. I mean he's portraying or reenacting something."

Montufar leaped from her chair and began pacing the edge of the room, her expression twisted into a scowl of concentration. "Brilliant. Crazy, but brilliant. How about this? He joins the military, lives through a series of traumatic experiences, ends up with PTSD. PTSD patients are known to relive their experiences in nightmares. Do they ever relive them through reenactment?"

The others said nothing, none of them being an expert on the subject, but it wasn't hard to see where she was going.

"I expect that would be quite a chore," Peller said. "Tracking down all Iraq and Afghanistan veterans in Maryland who may have PTSD, whether diagnosed or not. And that's just taking into account recent history. What if he was in Vietnam? Hell, he could have been in Korea."

"That would make him pretty old," Dumas said dubiously.

"True, but all you need to shoot somebody is a steady hand and a good eye."

"At eighty? Rick, Korea veterans are—"

"Perhaps," Kaneko interrupted gently, "you could approach the problem from the other direction."

The detectives had almost forgotten the mathematician was there, so quiet was he. "Go on," Morris prompted.

"Perhaps you should inquire into Szwiec's military connections. If he was not in the military himself…" The mathematician glanced at Peller, who shook his head. "Then likely his contacts include only a few military personnel. If you can identify them, you may be led directly to Leo."

"Good point," Peller said. "Unfortunately, we've had a devil of a time trying to get any information at all on Szwiec." He leaned forward and extracted one of the folders from the mass of paper. Opening it, he scanned the contents and related the pertinent bits. "We know he dropped out of high school, got a driver's license and abused the privilege almost but not quite enough to have it suspended, and has worked a few low-end jobs. He doesn't seem to have any bank accounts. His parents divorced when he was nine; shortly thereafter his father was killed while driving drunk. Ran into a parked semi at high speed. His mother pulled a disappearing act right after Szwiec dropped out of high school. We haven't been able to find her. Since he dropped out of school, nobody's had any contact with him. No friends from school that he kept up with. No girlfriend. His neighbors didn't know him. It's almost like the guy didn't exist."

Dumas flipped his coin again. "And yet, somehow he knew Leo."

"Seems so," Peller agreed.

"You need to find his mother," Kaneko told them.

Dumas tossed the half-dollar from one hand to the other and performed a vanish. Again, not too bad. "We've tried," he said, sounding irritated. "Wherever she went, she didn't leave a trail. No current driver's license, no credit cards or bank accounts that we can find, no utility bills in her name. She might be dead for all we know."

Kaneko didn't press the matter, but his expression suggested he knew something the rest of them didn't, something he wasn't ready to share.

Peller didn't like that suggestion in the least.

Σ

While her husband talked with the detectives, Sarah Kaneko settled in with a cup of tea and the computer in her husband's office. There she busied herself with the case, sifting through the emails Tomio had received in reply to his inquiry. From these, she built an annotated list of students with notable mathematical talent who were known or thought to have joined the military. Twenty-seven emails had come in on the subject, most of which contained more than one candidate. Between logging each name along with contact information and whatever notes she could ferret out from the often rambling messages, she took sips of tea and pondered the randomness of the information.

John Halloran, majored in chemistry, a talented math student, joined the Air Force after graduation. Present status unknown.

Victor Alyabyev, a business major who stood out from the crowd in nearly every math class he took, joined the Marines a year before he was due to graduate. Killed by an IED in Iraq.

Krista Leandres, no declared major, showed considerable aptitude for math and had been encouraged by several professors to pursue it before she suddenly withdrew, enlisted in the army, and was deployed to Afghanistan. She returned home later, but didn't resume her studies. She may have married a fellow soldier, although that wasn't clear.

And so forth and so on. There were no common events connecting any two stories, and most of the professors had lost contact with their former students. A handful of students remained in the military; a few had risen in the ranks to become noncommissioned officers. One or two had transferred to other universities to complete their studies. Sarah was concerned about the vagueness of the information. It meant a lot of additional research, probably attempting to get close to the former students. She knew that the odds were against any of them being the killer, but a persistent feeling of foreboding insisted that she had already seen the killer's name. The premonition chilled her through, and the occasional sip of hot tea was powerless to warm her.

She saved the list, nearly complete now with sixty-one names on it, and went to put on a sweater.

Chapter 13

Although students are first taught to construct proofs by reasoning from what they know, often solutions are found through a process of elimination. But before that process can prove fruitful, one has to know the full set of possibilities. If the correct answer is not in your set of potential solutions, you will have a hard time finding it. Σ

What most bothered Peller as he drove up his street and pulled into his driveway was not that earlier that day Howard County's most wanted criminal had gunned down Howard County's second-most wanted criminal right in front of his house while half a dozen of his colleagues watched. That hadn't been pretty for the department, surely, but what really bothered him was that nobody could figure out where Leo had been hiding when he killed Szwiec. The evidence suggested the shot had come from a height, which meant either an upper floor or the roof of one of the nearby houses. Yet an extensive search of the area, conducted with considerable cooperation from the residents, had turned up no evidence of Leo's presence.

Peller killed the engine, got out, slammed the door a bit harder than usual, and walked to the front of his property. He gazed up and down the street as though some crucial bit of evidence might suddenly materialize before him, something that everyone else had missed, but naturally it didn't.

He mounted the steps to his front porch, grimaced at the broken window to the right where the officers had gained entry to search his place, and unlocked the door. Inside, he flipped on the light. The foyer looked exactly as it always looked. Stairs to the left, living room to the right, a couple of mountain landscapes decorating the walls, coat closet straight back.

In the living room, shattered glass littered the dark blue sofa that had been Sandra's last purchase for the household. That would be fun to clean up. Photos of Sandra, Jason, Belinda, Susie, and Andrew—both portraits and candid shots—hung on the walls. Nothing out of place here, either, except for the broken window.

He moved through the entire house, room by room, taking everything in as though it were a crime scene. Kitchen, dining room, family room, each of the three bedrooms, even the basement and the attic. Nothing. Well, almost nothing.

At first he felt as though he were a stranger here, as though it were not his house but someone else's, but the farther he went the more he became aware of memories lurking in every corner, peeking out from behind curtains and closet doors. The more he looked, the more they revealed themselves and the more he was forced to confront them. The table where so many family meals had been eaten, so many birthday candles had been blown out, so many games had been played. Jason's room, where once a crib had stood and where the trappings of infancy had gradually given way to those of childhood and adolescence. The bedroom he had shared with Sandra, still decorated in the floral prints and lace she had loved. The exact spot in the foyer where he had been standing when a pair of officers, both of whom he personally knew, told him she was dead.

Investigation forgotten, he felt compelled to revisit these memories room by room until all the ghosts had shown themselves and he had embraced each in turn. It left him more exhausted than he had ever felt. He dragged himself back to the living room, stared without comprehension at the broken glass glittering like miscast stars on the sofa and floor beneath the shattered window.

The secret, he had told rookie officer Sheila Crane, was to avoid thinking too hard about it. He liked to think himself strong enough to handle tragedy, but maybe he had just been looking the other way all this time.

Turning away from the window, his eyes were drawn to a photo of Sandra and Jason on the front porch swing. Jason had been just two years old then. Sandra's smile had lit up the whole neighborhood the day he took that picture. He remembered feeling that way as he depressed the shutter.

The picture was hanging off-kilter. Without a thought, he reached up and shifted it a bit to the right. As it moved, a scrap of paper fell out from behind it and fluttered to the floor. Unable to fathom where that had come from, he picked it up. On one side, it bore a message written in small, blocky letters, almost as though a child had written it.

Another firstborn son, then I give you three back.
Thanks for the use of your bedroom window.

Σ

Dumas arrived at Peller's house first, and after making sure his colleague was all right he infiltrated the kitchen and made coffee for them. Montufar, for once not operating at warp speed, entered just as he was pouring.

"Are you okay, Rick?" she asked. Dumas heard the concern in her voice, but Peller simply stared into his coffee. She laid a comforting hand on his shoulder before slipping into the chair beside him and picking up the note. "He left this?"

Dumas nodded and handed Montufar a full mug of coffee. She added two teaspoons of sugar from the red stoneware bowl at the center of the table. Dumas checked the refrigerator and found a half-pint of table cream. Like his grandmother, he drank café au lait. He added a heavy dose of cream and sugar to his coffee, put the half-full pot back on the warming plate, and joined his colleagues.

Peller silently warmed his hands on his mug. "You know what my retirement plans are?" he asked, watching the steam swirl up from his coffee.

"Denver," Montufar said quietly. "Where your family is." She looked around at the kitchen. There was a sort of old-fashioned stability to the room that brought a sense of calm to those who entered it, and she suspected that Peller must not have made any changes to it since his wife died. Her touch was everywhere—in the cheerful vintage crockery; the cherry-patterned, ruffled café curtains; the pristine tablecloth. She felt as though she had stepped into the 1950s, and wondered if Sandra had been recreating her own grandmother's kitchen. She suddenly had an overwhelming memory of her own grandmother's house: the rich scents of cooking, the warm colors, the love and security she had always felt there.

He nodded. "A few months after the accident I started thinking about selling the house, but then I realized that would just add to the emotional upheaval. I can't live someplace that has no..." He waved half-heartedly.

"Roots," Dumas suggested.

Peller nodded. "Roots." He took a sip and closed his eyes. "So I thought I'd wait until Jason's family had put them down." He opened his eyes and glared at the note. It seemed to accuse them silently. "Why me? What does he have against me?"

"Do you have any military connections?" Dumas asked.

"I know a few people who were in the armed forces years back. I don't think I know anyone who's currently in the military."

"That can't be it, then." Dumas grinned wickedly and nudged the sugar bowl towards Montufar. "If you want to stay somewhere else for a couple of days," he offered, "I have a spare room in my apartment."

Peller shook his head slightly. "Thank you, but no. I'm not about to even look like I'm running away."

Absently, Montufar pulled the sugar bowl closer and added another half-teaspoon to her coffee. "Do you belong to a church?" she asked abruptly, her eyes focused on something well beyond the room.

Peller regarded her, bemused. "When I was growing up, we went to a Methodist church. I fell out of the habit after I left home, though." He took a sip of his coffee while Montufar stirred hers. "Sandra was more of a find-Jesus-on-your-own type, so she was fine keeping what religion we did have in our home."

"My family's Catholic," Montufar said, finally looking at her companions. "I could make the Sign of the Cross before I could walk." Leaning back and gazing up at the ceiling, she let out a breath and shook her head. "But after all this, I have to wonder if God's listening."

Dumas found the utter exhaustion in her voice distressing. He seldom discussed religion. His thoughts on the subject tended toward the unorthodox even for these times, and such conversations didn't often turn out well. But Montufar needed some encouragement, so he ventured, "He is. Usually we're the ones who aren't."

Montufar gave him a long-suffering look, then turned it on Peller. When Peller smiled and raised his cup in salute, she burst out laughing.

"What?" Dumas asked.

"That's an awfully deep thought for you," she said, poking his shoulder. "But you may be right. My mom would certainly agree."

"So," Peller said, "what is it we're not listening to here?"

"It can't be an accident Leo's involved you," Montufar replied. "If we're right that he's reenacting events from his military service, in his mind you must represent something connected to those events."

Peller took a sip of his coffee and regarded her thoughtfully. "How would a cop figure into events like that?"

Dumas saw it in sudden flash, as though events were playing out before his eyes. The confusion of a war in which the enemy didn't wear a uniform, in which a house might harbor either innocents or combatants, in which snap judgments sometimes went horribly wrong, in which fear and anger muddled by confusion sometimes led to tragic mistakes and sometimes drove soldiers over the edge. "You represent the one who stopped him," he said. "Or the one who should have stopped him. He did something terrible over there, or he was closely involved when someone did something terrible, and whoever should have stopped it didn't. Now you have to."

From the looks Peller and Montufar gave him, he thought he must have just set a new record for crazy ideas. Yet it fit the picture of Leo they had been painting all this time.

Peller pushed his mug away. "If you're right, this could blow up in our faces. Whatever he did while deployed, it hasn't made the news. The military will want to keep it that way."

"That's the least of our concerns," Montufar said in an unusually subdued voice.

Dumas found her tone unnerving. Picking up the note and gazing at it to cover his reaction, he asked, "What do you mean?"

"Leo used Szwiec and disposed of him when he no longer needed him. He's using Rick, too."

Peller grimaced. "But he still needs me, Corina. The sequence isn't complete."

"And when it is?"

Peller had no answer for that, nor did Dumas. "I give you three back," Dumas read. "That's odd."

"It's a negative," Peller told him. "The next two numbers are one and negative three."

"We'd better give this to Tom right away."

Peller glanced at the clock on the wall to his right. "It can wait until morning. Let him get some sleep."

Montufar took a drink of her coffee. "Someone might as well," she said.

Σ

Sleep, however, was not on Kaneko's agenda just yet. The list of sixty-one names Sarah had assembled beckoned him. They fell into four broad categories: the deployed, the discharged, the disappeared, and the dead. The first and last held little interest for him. For the most part, the whereabouts of the discharged were known or easily ascertained, but only a fraction of them now resided in Maryland. The disappeared could be alive or dead, deployed or home, and if alive and home might live anywhere in the U.S. They had not truly disappeared. Their former professors simply didn't know what had become of them. And they comprised over half the list.

Kaneko, however, was a patient man. One had to be patient to be a mathematician, he mused, since one could spend a lifetime on the most abstruse—some might also say obtuse—problems with no guarantee of success. One also had to know how to look for patterns, not only in numbers but also in structures, and in this case he thought he could see a pattern in the structure of Leo's life. He saw a young man with both physical strength and intellectual gifts who had enlisted in the military, was involved in intense combat action, and came home mentally damaged. Thus, Kaneko reasoned, he would not be navy or air force. He would be army or marines. He would not have close family who would be concerned for him and care for him upon his return.

Having decided this much, Kaneko divided the list of those known to be in Maryland into likely and unlikely candidates. There were only four of the latter. This he would supplement with likely candidates from disappeared list, once he had located them.

And then, he thought, *we will see what we have. Let us hope the list remains short. If so, I will turn it over to Lieutenant Peller.*

Σ

One person in the department did manage a full night's sleep: Captain Morris. Her husband Daniel, a physician, took considerable pains to make sure his wife stayed healthy in spite of the stress of her job. The more stressful the days grew, the more protective he turned, so that recent evenings consisted of half-hour walks through their neighborhood, tea, and Marx Brothers films. Some might have thought it an odd combination, she supposed, but it worked and she was readily able to fall asleep afterward.

This particular night was interrupted only by a dream of which Morris could just remember fragments when she awoke in the morning. She had been at a party in a huge hall with hundreds of guests. The hall was nondescript—a bare empty space— and all the guests except two were anonymous.

The first was Peller. Uncharacteristically, he was the center of attention, holding forth on some topic that she could not quite discern. A crowd had gathered around him, oblivious to all but his voice. She couldn't understand what the fascination was.

The second guest she knew was a mutual friend of theirs—Blake Compton, an intense, wiry man who had been a mentor to both of them as they rose through the department's ranks. Compton had come to law enforcement late, after a lengthy career in the Marines, during which he had risen to the rank of a senior noncommissioned officer. Early in his tour of duty, while stationed in Vietnam, he had received the Navy Cross and the Purple Heart. When pressed for the reason he dodged the question, leaving Morris to wonder if his reticence had to do with modesty, national security, or the diffuse anger felt by so many veterans of that war.

In the dream, Compton stood next to Morris, listening to Peller. "He talks too much," he said, nodding at the younger man.

Morris laughed.

"Tell him I said hello."

"Aren't you staying?"

She turned to him, but he was gone, and Morris awoke, startled from sleep. She looked at the clock. Three twenty-seven. She looked at Daniel, sleeping soundly beside her. Draping an arm over him, she soaked up his warmth and was soon asleep again.

Σ

The hunter rose two hours before dawn on Wednesday, March ninth, ate a big bowl of cold cereal drowned in milk, downed a tall glass of orange juice and a large mug of hot coffee, and pulled on his clothes: camouflage pants and shirt and brown boots, but not the red jacket one was supposed to wear. During hunting season, the red jacket was meant to keep you from being shot by other hunters, but today there would be no other hunters, at least not unless they were hunting him. He had been careful, very careful, but he wasn't so stupid as to think that they might not be hard on his trail. It was only a matter of time.

As it had been before.

The whole problem, he mused as he checked over the ten-gauge shotgun he'd picked up at a gun show three months back in West Virginia, was that you couldn't tell the good guys from the bad guys. You just couldn't take chances. Everyone knew that, but everyone wanted to pretend that the white hats and the black hats literally wore white and black. It wasn't like that at all. Walk into a house and they're all there, black hats and white hats and gray hats and people who change hats to fit the prevailing style. There was only one way to deal with that.

Take this guy, this Alexis Chalmers. He was probably okay. But how could one know? He kept a very strict routine, cycling around the neighborhood every morning on his racing bike, always wearing those weird neon clothes that cyclists liked to wear, always taking the same route, up and down the same hills, carefully regulating his speed, timing himself. He could just be exercising or training for a race.

Then again. That Raheem fellow said he was just trying to make a living, a handyman repairing whatever needed fixing in people's homes and shops, and look how that had turned out. His real racket was selling information on troop locations and movements to terrorists. How many IED's were placed in just the right spots thanks to Raheem's "innocent" business?

Stuffing the gun into its carrying case, the hunter had to admit that on rare occasions he felt a bit sorry about that one. Not for Raheem, but for his old man. His old man legitimately did the sort of work Raheem did as a cover for treachery. He'd taught Raheem everything he knew about the business.

You'd think a firstborn son would have a little more respect.

$$\Sigma$$

The first item on Montufar's agenda that morning was visiting Eduardo. Her brother, still looking a bit wan, was awake enough to smile at her when she came through the door. She went quickly to his side and ran a hand lightly over his cheek. "How are you?" she asked, her voice as soft as it ever got.

He nodded weakly.

Recalling what Dr. Kendrick had said about the skull fracture and possible loss of verbal memory, she wondered if his silence was due to the injury or simply that he wasn't strong enough to speak yet. "Well, you're looking much better this morning," she told him. "Yesterday you looked like a car had run you over. Today you only look like it hit you."

Eduardo cracked a smile and chuckled, although the effort seemed a bit much for him. "Ella?" he asked.

"Once she knew you were going to pull through, she did, too."

"She needs a husband."

"You won't get off the hook that easily."

He chuckled again, then closed his eyes. "I'm not good company. Too tired." He peeked at her with one eye to see her reaction.

"Nonsense. You're more fun asleep than most people are awake."

He closed his eye again and smiled. "I know."

She held his hand for awhile and he drifted off to sleep. She could have stayed there all morning, but a few minutes later her cell phone began vibrating. Her throat constricted when she saw it was Peller.

Connecting, she asked, "What now?"

"How's Eduardo?" he asked.

"He's doing okay. Sleeping at the moment."

"I hate to do this, but the next victim's been found, a college student shot while cycling around Clarksville." He gave her the location and told her he was en route.

"All right, I'll be there as soon as possible." She hung up and looked at Eduardo's face, relaxed in sleep. Releasing his hand, she moved quietly to the door.

Just as she was about to leave, he spoke again, although his eyes remained closed. "Be careful."

"I will," she promised. "Get some sleep now."

But he already was.

Σ

Of all the strange things that had happened in this case, Dumas thought, this was the strangest. Of course he knew it had to do with the sequence of numbers, and

Leo had already told them what the next numbers were, but this was no less creepy for it.

The call had come in while Peller and Montufar were on their way to Clarksville. A woman in hysterics called 911, demanding that the police immediately surround her house to keep the killer out. "It's him!" she kept insisting. "It has to be him!" There was little doubt who she thought it was, so Dumas raced the three squad cars that had been dispatched to the cluster of houses on Woodlot Road near its intersection with Harper's Farm Road, not sure if he wanted to beat them there or not. On the one hand, it was probably foolish to wade in alone. On the other, he wouldn't mind being the one to take Leo down.

As it turned out, they all arrived at once. The houses, eight in all, huddled between the road and a stand of woods. They were largish homes, upper-middle-class in feel, all unique and yet in some odd way feeling like clones of each other. Four of them stood directly on Woodlot. A narrow lane cut between the middle two, giving access to four more behind, set in a semicircle. The call had come from the northernmost of these.

One of the uniformed officers accompanied Dumas while the others carefully moved around the outside of the house and, after determining it was clear, fanned out to check the other houses and the woods.

The door snapped open as soon as Dumas rang the bell, revealing the hysterical woman who had placed the call. "Oh my God!" she moaned. "Thank you, thank you! Oh my God!" She looked to be in her early sixties and was surprisingly short for the size of her voice, standing just under five feet tall.

"May we come in?" Dumas asked, keeping his expression calm but unsmiling.

She stepped back and motioned them in. "Yes, come in. It took you forever. Seemed like it anyway. This is horrible! Come here, let me show you this."

As she led them back through the foyer to a living room done up like an Italian villa, Dumas said, "I have to apologize, but I don't know your name. We were in a rush to get out here."

"Phyllis Waggoner," she replied. "I live here with my son Bernie and his wife Magda. Just look at this."

She picked up a slip of paper from the coffee table and handed it to Dumas. It appeared to be a fragment of college-ruled notebook paper, possibly ripped from a spiral notebook, bearing a message in carefully-penned block letters: **Three potential targets spared.**

"Where did you find this?" Dumas asked.

Waggoner pointed to the coffee table. "Right there. It's him, isn't it?" Her lips quivered as if she were about to cry, but she sucked in a breath and stared into Dumas' eyes as if challenging him to say anything different.

He nodded. "It is. But I don't think you need to worry. He's basing his crimes on numbers, and today's number was negative three. He picked you because three people live here, three people who he did not intend to kill."

"But he was here. He was standing right here in this room, in this spot, when he left that note."

"He won't be back," Dumas said. "I think we can be sure of that."

Sinking to the sofa, Waggoner watched Dumas bag the note and instruct the officer to call in the crime scene unit. "How?" she asked.

"It's how he works. He never targets the same place twice. He mixes things up, tries to keep us on our toes. We're going to have our people go over your house to see if we can find any material evidence. Fingerprints, that sort of thing."

She nodded absently. Just as Dumas turned to leave, she said, "He mixes things up? Then maybe this time he *will* come back!"

Chapter 14

I've frequently found that the hardest problems are solved not through incessant work but by feeding the mind and then letting it rest. How often has a breakthrough been made not at the whiteboard or the computer but over dinner, in the shower, or even through a dream. The subconscious is always at work, and it works best when left on its own.

Unfortunately, when people are dying we are reluctant to take a break. When stumped, Sherlock Holmes gave himself the luxury of smoking his pipe, but we do no such thing lest people think we are not taking the matter seriously. Do more people live as a result? Or do more people die? Σ

Wednesday afternoon, once the crime scene work was done and the detectives were back at headquarters, Captain Morris called them together again in the conference room and closed the door—rather more pointedly than usual, Peller thought. "So where do we stand now?" she asked.

"Up against the wall," Peller replied. "He's like a ghost. He comes and goes as he pleases, leaves no trace except for dead bodies, and only tells us enough about his plans to drive us mad."

"You're saying we know nothing."

"Nothing of any use."

"Not quite true," Dumas objected. "We're pretty sure he's military or ex-military and has enough mathematical training to know how to construct the number sequences he's been using. We think he's somehow reenacting events he lived while deployed. The military might actually know about him, about things he did that they don't want known."

"Most of that's speculation," Peller replied. "Even if it's true it doesn't help us identify or apprehend him."

Morris directed an impatient gaze at Montufar, who shook her head.

"I'm afraid Rick's right. We can put together enough to have a vague picture of Leo, but he's been too careful. We can't get near him."

"What about Tom?" the captain asked. "Has he come up with anything helpful so far? Where is he, anyway?"

"We have to give him the new numbers," Dumas said.

"Do that. What else? There must be something we can do."

Peller leaned back. "Only thing I can think of is to contact the military. But as Eric said, they may not want us digging too far into Leo's background." Morris scowled at him, then looked away. He couldn't blame her for being frustrated and angry with her crew. They should have had some results by now, at least a suspect or two, but all they could produce were a few educated guesses. And the killings went on.

To underscore the point, the youngest detective on the force, a twenty-six year old Cherokee woman named Holly Ross, poked her head into the room and made a "phone call" gesture at Peller. "It's him," she said.

"Send it in here," Morris said before Peller could speak. When the phone rang a moment later, he put it on speaker.

"You're doing well," Leo said, his voice sounding distant and strained.

"My boss doesn't agree," Peller replied. "She thinks I should have you in irons by now."

"She doesn't appreciate your talents the way I do."

"What do you want?"

"The ground floor, then building thirty-three. I'll give you the final number tomorrow."

There had been seven numbers in the initial sequence, and with the two just received they had six in the new sequence. The meanings of the numbers in the new sequence matched exactly to those in the first, so Peller knew what was coming: tomorrow's number would be some number of victims. But would a third sequence start, or was the end of this sequence Leo's real purpose?

"And then what?" Peller asked.

Leo's breathing remained unchanged, but he took a moment to reply. "Then we will see. I fear our relationship may be short-lived. A pity, really. I find I rather like you."

Before Peller could reply, the connection was cut. He ran a hand through his hair and looked around at his colleagues.

"He's going to disappear into the night," Dumas said. "He's going to finish this sequence and vanish. We're going to have a pile of bones and no justice for any of them."

"He wants to," Montfar said. "But he's not sure. In spite of everything, he thinks we might catch him."

Morris directed a sour look at the ceiling. "I agree with Rick. We need contact the military. We need to see if they can give us any names. Even if we have to obscure Leo's background for public consumption, we need a name."

Peller wasn't at all sure it would help, but he knew none of them had a better idea. "You have any likely contacts?"

The captain pondered. "Not directly, but I think I can manage it. Which reminds me—I saw Blake Compton last night."

"Blake?" Peller was astonished. "I thought he was dead—didn't he die up in Maine a couple of years ago? Not too long after he retired?"

She nodded absently. "It was in a dream. Some big gathering or another. He was there. He said to tell you hello. So hello from Blake. Weirdest dream I've ever had, and so real." Sitting forward, she said, "I'll try to get us a contact. You call Tom and give him the latest numbers. We have to figure this out before Leo drops off the face of the Earth."

It wasn't until Peller was sitting down at his desk that he remembered. Six years ago Blake Compton's retirement party had been held at the Columbia Sheraton. It was a big gathering, drawing in police and military personnel he had worked with over the years. The Pentagon had sent some big-name general to speak, and Peller had been asked to speak for the department. The event had been covered in all the local papers, the *Baltimore Sun*, and the city TV stations. It was a great local story: wounded war hero retires from outstanding career in law enforcement, covered head to toe in stars and bars.

Leo, had he not been overseas at the time, would have heard about it. Peller nearly bolted from his chair, intending to pass this along to Morris, but the phone rang before he could take two steps. He snatched up the receiver and snapped, "Peller."

"I'm calling about my son," the caller said. The woman sounded hesitant, as though wishing she hadn't placed the call but having done so was committed to seeing it through.

"Your son?"

"Yes. I saw it on TV this morning. He's . . ." She choked back a sob. "They killed him."

Confused, Peller asked as gently as he could, "What's his name?"

"Julian," she said. "Julian Szwiec."

Σ

The telephone book might be approaching obsolescence, Kaneko mused, but it still had its uses. It had quickly shown that a handful of his "missing persons" were alive and well in the area. Between that, and a few phone calls and internet searches, he had satisfied himself that the list of eleven now on the desk before him represented the most likely candidates for Leo. If the prevailing assumptions were correct, at any rate.

He considered taking the list directly to Detective Lieutenant Peller and removing himself from the investigation, but it bothered him that it was so large. It shouldn't have, he knew. The police had the resources to check on eleven people, surely. Still, this wasn't a solution. It was merely a set of possible solutions. How could a mathematician be satisfied with that?

The whisper of shoes against the carpet signaled Sarah's approach. He turned and looked up at her, his expression apparently giving away his thoughts.

"You've finished," she said.

"I have a list."

"And is that the finish?"

He picked up the paper and studied it.

She sighed and held out a hand. "Let me see." He passed it to her and she looked it over: names, addresses, phone numbers. "How do you want to go about this?"

"I thought I might call them. I can use the same story I gave my colleagues. I can find out more about their military experiences and what they've been doing since returning home."

"Nobody is going to admit to a killing spree." She handed the list back.

"Of course not. But they might give details that can be checked. At best we might catch the killer in a lie. At worst, we might get a feeling for the most likely suspects."

"No. At worst we might be killed."

He pondered that for a moment. Death didn't frighten him particularly, but certainly he would not want to expose Sarah to unnecessary danger. "Should I use a false name?"

"Let me call," she said. "I'll identify myself as a research assistant at the university."

Kaneko rose and wrapped his wife in his arms. "I don't know how you put up with me," he said. "But I must be the luckiest man in the world."

"Let's see how this ends before we decide how lucky you are," she said and gave him a peck on the cheek.

A moment later they were interrupted by a phone call from Eric Dumas, who had two new numbers to report.

Σ

Peller wanted to check newspaper archives for stories about Blake Compton's retirement party, so he sent Montufar to talk with Debra Szwiec, Julian's mother. In spite of their inability to locate her before she called, she was surprisingly close by, living some twenty-five miles to the west in an apartment complex on the northwest edge of Frederick.

After a courtesy call to the Frederick police department, Montufar made a beeline to the apartment. When Mrs. Szwiec opened the door, Montufar was confronted with an almsost-skeletal woman with deep-shadowed eyes, whose trembling fingers seemed barely able to keep hold of a cigarette. Montufar introduced herself and the woman let her into an apartment that was immaculate but had an air of faded neglect, as though its occupant simultaneously suffered from an obsessive disorder that kept her scrubbing and vacuuming long after it was necessary, but was long past caring where she was.

"Would you like some coffee?" Mrs. Szwiec asked as they seated themselves on a frayed sofa.

Montufar declined. "Tell me about your son."

"Julian's father died in a crash," she said, her eyes looking everywhere but at her visitor. "His name was Frank and he was a drunk. I divorced him when Julian was nine. I never should have married him in the first place, but you know how it goes. We were involved in high school and everything was just great fun then. After Julian was born, it went to hell. I guess it was going that way even before. Frank was drunk half the time, then most of the time, then finally all the time. He'd hit me when he was mad and try to rape me when he wasn't. Since he was drunk, that usually didn't go to well for him." She forced a laugh, but it came out more a pathetic bark.

"What happened after the accident?" Montufar asked, trying to sound sympathetic. She had never understood why a woman would stay in a situation like that. Why put up with nine years of hell before getting out?

Mrs. Szwiec shrugged. "Julian was about grown up. He'd dropped out of high school and made it pretty clear he wanted to live life his own way, without mommy interfering. He moved in with a friend and I said to hell with it and left." She picked at her nails. "That sounds like I didn't love him. I did. I just didn't know what to do with him anymore."

"I'm sorry things turned out this way," Montufar told her sincerely. She pitied this woman, pitied her pain and her empty life. "Maybe he fell in with the wrong people. We don't know because we haven't been able to find out much about him. We only know that the last person he thought was his friend killed him. Do you know any of the people in his circle?"

Mrs. Szwiec stubbed out her cigarette and lit another. Montufar, who had not grown up around smokers and felt ill at the smell, tried hard to keep hold of her lurching stomach. "He was a loner. The other kids pushed him around and made fun of him. I don't think he had many friends, certainly not before I left. The only guy he hung out with at all as far as I know was the guy he moved in with. I think his name was Larry Fry or something like that. He was pretty good-looking and always seemed to have a couple of girls hanging around him, but I thought he was a creep. At the time I wondered if that was why Julian hung out with him. The girls all hated Julian. Maybe they saw something I couldn't see. I wondered if maybe this Larry guy got him some action. Some girls, they'll do anything if the price is right."

"Any idea where this Larry Fry lives?"

"Hon, I've been out here a few years now. I don't know where anyone from back then would be." Her last cigarette had gone to ash, and she reached for the pack again.

"Did you try to keep in touch with him? Or any of the other members of your family? We couldn't find any trace of you before you called. It was like you'd vanished off the face of the earth."

"You're probably wondering why I even bothered." Mrs. Szwiec studied the glowing tip of her cigarette for a moment before continuing. "You're out of your jurisdiction, so I suppose it's okay to tell you. I don't use my real name anymore, and I live on a cash basis. No bank account, no credit cards. I don't even have a current driver's license. I make what money I can servicing men who are as sick as Frank was, each in his own way. Seems I couldn't get away from him even after he died."

She cast a quick glance at Montufar as though to gauge the detective's reaction, but there wasn't any. Montufar kept her gaze level and didn't as much twitch.

"Anyway," she continued after another drag on her cigarette, "I did have one reason to call you. When you're done with him, I want Julian's body so I can give him a decent burial."

$$\Sigma$$

The scanned papers that Peller reviewed had all carried essentially the same story. He was surprised at how often his name appeared in the articles. He had given a short speech at Compton's retirement party, and snippets of it had been repeated by the press. In their version, what he remembered as a fairly short and simple tribute to a man who had given the county years of devoted service had been exaggerated until it sounded like a eulogy delivered by a loving son. Or maybe he only thought that because death was so much in the air of late.

It took Peller no time at all to realize that Leo could have gotten his name from any of these stories. The military connection seemed telling, assuming their hypothesis was correct, but it remained mere hypothesis. Two possibilities still existed: either Leo knew him personally, or Leo had found him through the news. He thought the former unlikely, but the latter was just plain odd unless Leo had somehow also known Compton. In the depths of Leo's mind, did he identify Peller with Compton? And if he did, why?

"Excuse me, Detective Peller."

Peller looked up with a start to find Kaneko standing by his desk, a worried look on his face. "Oh, Tom. Sorry. I just learned something that may be important. Or it may not. I wish I knew which."

"Are you no closer to Leo than before?" The question was asked timidly, almost awkwardly, as though it had to be asked but Kaneko didn't want to give it voice.

"Afraid not. Have a seat." Peller waved to a chair next to his desk. "How about you?"

Kaneko sat, his posture perfect. "Detective Dumas sent me the latest numbers. Using them, I've been able to determine the sequence Leo is using."

It sounded to Peller's ears like the best news he'd heard since the whole business began. He knew that was irrational—knowing the sequence would be of little help—but he desperately needed something to hang onto. "So what are we dealing with?" he asked.

"I told you before that the Fibonacci sequence is generated by a complementary pair of Lucas sequences. The sequence Leo is using now is also generated by a complementary pair of Lucas sequences. It's easy to generate such a sequence if you know the rules. You can set up a spreadsheet to do it for you. All you need are the seed numbers, but I won't bore you with the details. The numbers we have are two, three, one, negative three, one, and thirty-three. The next number, I'm afraid, is one hundred nine."

Peller sat back, the good feeling gone. "One hundred nine?"

"Yes. And it refers, like the original sequence, to the number of victims."

Peller felt as though he were trapped in a nightmare. "My God. But like you said before, how do you manage to kill exactly the right number of people when the number is that large?"

The mathematician shuddered. "I don't want to know."

Peller remembered that he was talking to a man whose life experiences included the death of tens of thousands. He stared blankly at his computer screen for a few moments. The background noise of the office—people talking, phones ringing, the hum of the heating system—failed to mask the sounds of the two men breathing.

"What have you just learned?" Kaneko asked.

Peller turned back to the monitor, where the scanned story waited patiently. "Well, about six or seven years ago, Blake Compton retired from the force. He'd been in the Marines, won medals in Vietnam, all kinds of awards from the police force. When Captain Morris and I were rookies, he took us under his wing and made sure we didn't screw up too much. Anyway, when he retired there was a big party, and I made a farewell speech that the papers picked up. They ran my name along with his. So I wondered if—" A thought sprang from his subconscious mind, dark and deadly.

Retirement party. There were so many people.

Party.

"Yes?" the mathematician prompted.

"A party! Damn it! I know what he's doing!"

Kaneko leaned forward, his expression intense.

"How do you kill exactly one hundred nine people? By attacking a gathering of exactly one hundred nine people. A gathering where the guest list is known in advance. Something like a retirement party!" He turned the monitor to face Kaneko.

Kaneko skimmed the story. "Yes," he said. "That makes sense. Do you think Leo knew Blake Compton?"

"No way to know yet," the detective replied. "But I do think this is how he got my name, and I do think it suggests we're on the right track with the military connection."

"Ex-Marines would be weighted higher as suspects, then."

Peller looked at Kaneko, sensing that there was something the mathematician hadn't told him yet. But the other quietly resumed an upright pose, looked away, and said nothing. "If you know something, or even just suspect something," Peller told him, "now would be a good time to let us know."

Kaneko shook his head. "It's nothing but a hunch. If Leo is recreating events from his armed forces days, it seems likely he would have been in the Army or Marines rather than the Navy or Air Force. Blake Compton was in the Marines, according to the news article."

Peller considered this for a moment. It made sense, but they were still piling speculation upon speculation. "I just wish we could get to a real name. Or even five real names."

"Yes," Kaneko agreed. "That would indeed be helpful."

∑

From her husband's home office, Sarah Kaneko quickly worked through the list of eleven suspects, calling them each and delivering her prepared speech.

"I'm calling on behalf of a research study being conducted by the mathematics department at Johns Hopkins University in Baltimore. We're interested in talking with former students who either majored in mathematics or received significant mathematics instruction at the University and later served in the military to study the contributions of higher education in mathematics to our nation's armed forces. We were wondering if you would be willing to participate in such a study?"

If the suspect answered affirmatively, she proceeded to ask a few questions: How many hours of mathematics instruction did you receive? What was the most advanced mathematics course you took? What branch of the service were you in? What was your reason for enlisting? Did you utilize any of your mathematics training while serving? If so, in what way? Are you available to answer follow-up questions if needed?

Of the eleven, four declined to answer and seven answered all questions in what she thought was a reasonable manner. But there had been one peculiar moment. After Sarah had recited her speech to suspect number six, for a heartbeat or two all she could hear was him drawing in a breath, slowly, deliberately, as though he had to gauge whether or not she was who she said she was. But then he said, "Yes, of course. I'd be glad to help," and the rest of the conversation was as uneventful as any other.

At the end of the call, she tapped her pen on the suspect's name, wondering how much to make of it. Maybe at first he just hadn't been sure whether to take part. Four others had declined, after all. Finally, she circled the name and moved on to the next call.

∑

The fiftyish African-American man who came through the door of the Pork Barrel restaurant just off of U.S. 40 and looked around as though searching for someone was former U.S. Representative Ralph Arriola, and he was indeed looking for someone. Captain Morris spotted him from her booth off to his left and waved until he noticed.

"With a name like Pork Barrel, this place should be in D.C.," he said as he slipped onto the bench opposite her.

"I think their original restaurant is down there," she replied. "They just opened this one last year. It's been awhile. How've you been?"

"Much better since I got out of politics."

Morris laughed. "I hear you lost a few friends when you decided not to run for reelection."

He waved that off with a crooked smile as the waitress approached. They both ordered coffee and Arriola asked for a slice of pecan pie. Perhaps sensing a poor tip, the waitress narrowed her eyes menacingly before moving off.

Arriola watched her go. "So what's the trouble?"

"Why does it have to be trouble?"

"Don't play games with me, Whitney. I read the news like everyone else."

Morris leaned forward, arms folded on the table, and regarded him with more than a little curiosity. She had known Arriola for about ten years. A successful local businessman, he had launched several companies in fields ranging from office furniture to medical practice business support and had easily won election to the House of Representatives, where he served two terms before deciding to quit. His straightforward manner no doubt had been a key factor in that. Always insisting upon having all the cards on the table, he had little patience for political games.

"This is strictly confidential," she told him quietly, and he nodded. "We think these killings are the work of a former soldier. He's probably psychologically disturbed and may be recreating incidents from his experience overseas. We need some help looking into who might fit the bill."

The waitress reappeared with the coffee and Arriola's pie. "Anything else?" she asked hopefully.

Arriola smiled up at her. "We're good for now, thanks." The smile might have given her a bit of hope. At any rate, she didn't make a face this time before moving on. Arriola took his time adding sugar to his coffee and stirring.

"Can you put me in touch with someone at DoD?" Morris finally asked.

"I can, but I doubt it will do you any good. You need to nail this guy yourselves, and if what you suspect about him is true, you'd best keep it quiet. Find another explanation for the public."

"I can't believe you just said that. You, of all people."

"I'm not saying I like it. I'm saying that's how it is." He jabbed a fork into his pie, twisted off a bite and looked at it as though it were trying to bite back. "The powers that be have a hard enough time dealing with the avalanche of bad PR that's fallen on them over the past ten years. You know what will happen if this gets out. Everyone from the commanders on the ground up to the President himself will be a target, and the VA will be dragged kicking and screaming into it, too. Again. You think they're going to help you find a soldier who went psycho over there and came back to recreate over there over here?"

"You're not saying anything we haven't already considered. Just get me a contact. Please."

"Your department needs you."

"Ralph!"

"I'm not kidding. You don't know when to quit, do you?"

Exasperated, Morris sat back and stared out the window. It was a sunny afternoon; a few cumulus clouds floating lazily by while beneath them the humans scurried about in their cars on their way to whatever business they thought they had. "People are dying."

"People are always dying." When her head snapped around and she fixed him with a fiery glare, he threw up his hands. "Okay, fine, I'll see what I can do."

"Thank you."

Arriola shoved his plate back, appetite apparently gone. "You can have that if you want. Leave a good tip." He rose and strolled off, looking more casual than he must have felt.

Morris watched him go out the door, then pulled the plate to herself and sampled the pie. Not bad, she thought. Not the best, but not bad.

Chapter 15

Chess-playing computers encounter an issue known as the horizon problem. Because the program can only look ahead a finite number of moves, it will push trouble out beyond the "horizon" to which it can see. In certain circumstances this causes it to be oblivious to impending trouble.

Human beings may suffer from a horizon problem of their own, but in their case it results from emotional factors, not computational limitations. Therapists call it "denial." Σ

It was still dark when the hunter set out on the morning of Thursday, March tenth, to finish his preparations. He hadn't thought of it before, but he now realized that everything up to this point had been just that: preparations for the one event that really mattered. The earlier operations and the one he was about to embark upon now all represented collateral damage necessary to his real purpose. Disturbing, yes, but couldn't it be said that war was always thus? Over sixty million people had died in World War II, and what was that but collateral damage resulting from the necessity of ridding the world of a single man's delusion?

The temperature was in the lower forties; the sky overcast and shedding a light drizzle as he stepped out of his small house and got into his car. Although still a hunter, he was dressed today in the camouflage of suburbia: jeans, a khaki button-down shirt, lightweight blue waterproof coat. He didn't look like he was hiding and thus would be perfectly hidden.

His weapon of choice today was a Browning Hi-Power, a classic handgun that had set him back a fair bit but was beautiful to behold. It fit nicely in his coat pocket. He intended to annoy Peller one last time by using it in back-to-back killings. Peller wouldn't know that it wasn't truly a break in the pattern, that both killings were actually part of a single operation.

In fact, he doubted that Peller understood the significance of the pattern. The hunter had taken great care in avoiding repetition early on. Once Peller had figured out the numbers, the numbers became the focus of attention, and it was easier to avoid detection. But a certain element of randomness remained critical. This was war, after all, and war is never neat and predictable. His re-creation had to reflect that reality.

Like his house, the hunter's car was unpretentious: a four-year-old Honda Civic, light gray, not too recently washed. It wouldn't call attention to itself. Even if it was seen in the target area, nobody would likely remember it. That was particularly important today, as the target area was the Columbia Crossing shopping center, a sprawl of commercial outlets lined with parking lots. It reminded him of a bustling Iraqi market in which his squad had foiled a coordinated suicide attack, or two-thirds of it at any rate. Acting on intelligence, they had spotted two of the three young men slipping into the crowd and had taken them out before anything could happen. But the third panicked, fled to the opposite end of the market, and in a pointless act of desperation detonated his device, killing not only himself but twelve others, all his own people.

Today's foray would be a small, imperfect, yet key reenactment of that event, completing the pattern. The hunter had done more to protect his country and its interests than any soldier he knew. As much as the powers that be wanted to pretend he didn't exist, they would not be allowed. He might die in the process, but they would, at last, be forced to acknowledge his contributions.

$$\Sigma$$

Everything struck at once, at five minutes before nine o'clock in the morning. Word reached Dumas about a pair of fatal shootings at the Columbia Crossing shopping center just as Montufar was beginning to brief him on her talk the previous afternoon with Debra Szwiec. As the two of them rose to leave, Captain Morris bustled through, accompanied by a dapper-looking Ralph Arriola and an immaculately turned-out Marine officer. She whisked them into her office and closed the door, but not before Dumas and Montufar spied the glint of stars at the officer's shoulder and sleeve.

Peller arrived just as his colleagues were leaving and stopped them at the edge of the parking lot. His eyes were red, with deep circles beneath them.

"What happened to you?" Montufar asked. "Didn't you get any sleep last night?"

"I spent most of last night digging up information on Blake Compton. It keeps getting worse," he told them. "Tom figured out the sequence. The next number is one hundred nine. I'm almost certain Leo means to stage an attack on a planned gathering. Could be a military retirement event like this one." He shoved copies of the news articles on Compton's retirement party into their hands.

But there was no time for discussion. Montufar drove while Dumas hung on, and shortly they were at the scenes of the crimes.

One shooting—the first to occur, according to witnesses—had taken place just inside the door of the office supply store near the north end of the complex. Montufar took charge of that scene, wondering what kind of strange thought process made Leo call this a killing on the ground floor when it took place in a one-story building.

The victim, a young black man dressed for a day at the office, had just entered the store. The shot came from outside, shattering the door's glass and leaving its victim sprawled face-down in the entrance. The officers who had questioned available witnesses came up empty-handed. Nobody had seen the shooter. Montufar suspected Leo had made the shot while sitting in his car.

The scene of the second shooting, which Dumas was investigating, had taken place at an art gallery at the south end of the complex. Almost diametrically opposed to the office supply store, its address was 33 Columbia Crossing Circle, the sixth number in Leo's sequence.

It was a good jaunt from one store to the other—over two and a half football fields, Dumas estimated. According to witnesses who heard both shots, the timings of the shootings were close—too close together to allow a man to run, much less walk, from one site to the other. Ergo, Leo must either have driven or fired both shots from somewhere in the middle of the parking lot. The latter seemed unlikely. He would have had to perch on top of a car, but nobody could be found who had seen him. So Dumas also concluded that Leo must have made the shots from within his car.

The victim at the gallery was an employee, a young Hispanic man who had just started work there the previous week. It had been a dream job for him, as he was studying art history at UMBC and, according to his boss, had loved being able to spend time among the paintings and other wares. The shot had taken him out while he was setting up a new arrival in the window display: a landscape by local artist Virginia Smullyan.

That name brought Dumas up short. Smullyan had been a witness connected with the murder of Roger Harrison. She had given Peller the one detailed description they had of Leo. He made a note to run this by Montufar as soon as possible. It was probably just an oddball coincidence, but it was decidedly oddball.

$$\Sigma$$

When Captain Morris emerged from her office and bid her visitors goodbye, she looked haggard. Peller had been keeping an eye on the proceedings from his desk while reviewing one more time everything they knew about Leo's killing spree, searching for some small detail he might have overlooked that would lead to the killer's identity. But there wasn't anything. A few pieces of information hadn't come his way yet— what Debra Szwiec had told Montufar, the details of this morning's murders—but he doubted anything would materialize. He even searched for information on upcoming gatherings in the area, checking newspapers and online announcements and even calling several banquet halls in the area, but to no avail. Parties were on the books, to be sure, but all of them either too large or too small to be Leo's intended target.

He waved Morris over and waited while she crossed the room and sank into the chair next to his desk. Their eyes silently communicated their shared exhaustion. Peller spoke first.

"I think we need to hold another press conference. Tell the public what we think is going to happen next. Ask for help in identifying likely targets."

Morris closed her eyes.

"I know," he replied to her unspoken objection. "But I don't think we have any other choice."

"Do you know who I was just talking to?" she asked, opening her eyes and regarding him with a defeated look.

Peller shook his head. He knew Ralph Arriola from news photos, but the military fellow was a stranger to him.

"Good," she said. "I'm not supposed to mention he was here. Although if he's trying to be secretive, why would he march in here all decked out like that? Ridiculous. The upshot of our conversation—if you could call it that—was that of course these crimes could not be the work of a U.S. soldier, and even breathing the suggestion was well-nigh treasonous."

"They're not even going to look into the possibility?"

Morris shook her head. "I got the feeling that more was going on behind that general's eyes than he let on. It occurs to me that should the Pentagon suspect who Leo is, they could very easily make him go away."

Peller straightened and pondered that for a moment. "You think they know?"

"Not yet. But I think they might be worried. This meeting wasn't about how they could help us. It was damage assessment. That's why they agreed so quickly to meet with me. They wanted to know everything we know, and they wanted to drop a few hints that if our suspicions pan out we should be careful what we make public."

"The military has no authority in this."

"No. But they could pull some strings and make their displeasure known. Ralph all but told me my professional head would be on the block if I stepped too far out of line."

Peller didn't consider himself to be naïve, not at his age and with his life experience, but he found it hard to swallow the idea that the military had much sway over county politics. Still, he wouldn't want his boss to be tossed out on her ear for doing her job.

"If worse comes to worst," he said, "I'll be happy to take the heat for you. I could probably do it under the radar, and I have a place to go if need be."

Morris smiled as much as her tired face could. "Much appreciated," she said, "but I don't think it will be necessary. I've been around the block a few times. I think I can play their game well enough."

She rose slowly and gazed toward the window. "About that press conference. Let's wait to see what Corina and Eric bring back. If need be we'll do it this afternoon, but it's our option of last resort."

Σ

Kaneko sat in his study, considering Sarah's list. She had given him a summary of what she had learned and pointed out the circled name. Then she put it in his hand, kissed him, and was out the door to meet some friends for lunch.

Something about her premonition niggled at him. He told himself that it was a very small thing: a moment's hesitation, nothing more. But what if it *were* something more? He thought of his mother's trip away from doomed Nagasaki. She had never been very specific in the reasons she gave him once he was old enough to understand— simply that she had not visited his grandparents for quite some time, and felt that it was time for her to do so. Had she sensed, somehow, what lay in the future?

He was a mathematician and did not deal in premonitions or intuition. Yet he lived today because of his mother's decision.

But such speculation was useless. There was work to be done. He turned to his file on the case and quickly located the information he had compiled on suspect number six. Once an engineering student with strong mathematical aptitude—according to a professor who had taught him in his junior year—Number Six had enlisted in the Marines immediately after graduating. He had briefly contacted the professor upon returning from an overseas tour of duty and asked for connections to help him find a job. The professor had obliged with three names, then heard nothing further. At Kaneko's request he followed up and learned that the student had never contacted the three.

Curious, Kaneko thought. There could be multiple valid explanations. Then again. . . .

He considered calling Peller, but he wasn't satisfied that he had anything useful to tell him. It warranted a closer look first. Having decided on a course of action, Kaneko quickly prepared an official-looking folder containing a data sheet on the suspect's educational and military background and his answers to the phone survey. He carefully omitted personal information such as name and address, but wrote the address down on a sticky note and tucked it into his left pants pocket. He selected a pen and a pad of paper from his desk, and, satisfied that he was prepared, set off for a face-to-face interview with Lucas Freiberg.

Σ

The homecoming was anything but triumphal. Peller thought that Montufar and Dumas looked like something the cat didn't consider worth dragging in. There was no point in asking how they'd fared. Leo hadn't left anything helpful in his wake. He came, he killed, he vanished, twice in the space of just a few minutes. People heard the shots, saw the victims drop, but of the assailant they saw no trace. Several witnesses, scared out of their wits, said it reminded them of the Beltway sniper attacks back in 2002 in which the fatal shots had been fired through a hole drilled in the trunk of a car.

The detectives reviewed the new information, such as it was, but nothing emerged from it. Peller then asked Montufar to recount her interview with Debra Szwiec and listened carefully until she mentioned Julian's friend, Larry Fry.

"Hold on," he said, leaning forward. "We've heard that name before."

Dumas scrolled through the files on the computer. "Have we?" he asked. "It does sound familiar. Here we go. Not Larry Fry, Luke Frey. I don't believe it."

Montufar sprang up and began pacing. "He's the guy who identified the golfer. He said that the golfer must live in his neighborhood!" She stopped dead and looked at Dumas. "My God, he was on the *phone* with Szwiec when we got there! Do you remember what he said, Eric?"

Dumas closed his eyes in concentration. "Something about a cousin of his who was always getting into trouble. On the phone he called him an idiot and said it was the last time he was going to help him out." He looked up at Montufar. "It's him. It's got to be him."

Peller felt their excitement, too, but it wasn't so conclusive to his mind. "Julian's mother called Frey a friend, not a cousin. His mother would know who his cousins were. This could just be a coincidence—two people with similar names."

"Have you noticed?" Montufar asked suddenly. "*All* the names in this case are similar. Leo, Larry, Lucas—like those families where all the kids have the same initials. Even Leonardo of Pisa, aka Fibonacci. We can't ignore it."

"I agree," Dumas said. "If we don't move on this and Tom is right about the next number . . ."

The thought hung between them like a cloud of chlorine gas.

"All right," Peller decided. "Let's get some backup and pay Mr. Frey a visit." Just as he rose, the phone rang.

"Leave it," Dumas suggested, but Peller snatched it up anyway and announced himself.

"Last number," Leo's familiar voice said.

Peller fought down the urge to drop Frey's name. Instead, he said, "One hundred nine."

Leo's breathing filled his ears. For a moment it seemed the only sound in the universe. Then the voice came again. "I'm impressed. But unfortunately for you, that's the easy part. And you've only just gotten that far, haven't you? Goodbye, Detective Lieutenant Peller. I doubt we shall speak again."

Peller managed to say, "Don't get your hopes up," before the connection was cut. He replaced the receiver.

Montufar and Dumas stood silent. "Come on," Peller told his colleagues. "Let's see if we got it right."

Chapter 16

That was, without doubt, the most foolish thing I've ever done. Σ

Kaneko had a GPS unit in his car, but he seldom used it. He preferred to check maps and get directions online so he knew where he was going before he set out. Today was no different. He located Woodland Road in Columbia at the eastern end of Centennial Park, noted how to get there from his home in Baltimore, neatly penned a couple of notes so he wouldn't forget the route, and set out.

When he arrived, he found a collection of about twenty squat houses huddled like toadstools in a clearing in the woods on the west side of the road along a series of unnamed drives. The houses seemed to face every which way, as though the streets. had been added as an afterthought.

Lucas Freiberg's house was one of those that backed up against the trees of the park. It was small, tan, and white-shuttered. A gray Honda Civic sat in the driveway. The neighborhood was quiet as Kaneko got out of his car and carefully closed the door. Birdsong and the faint rush of distant traffic was all he could hear.

Kaneko rang the doorbell and waited, the folder he had prepared saddled in the curled fingers of his left hand.

The man who opened the door fit Kaneko's idea of a Marine: tall and solid, clean-shaven, his hair close-cropped. His mouth was working as though chewing a stick of gum. Giving the mathematician a measured once-over, he said, "What can I do for you?"

"I'm from Johns Hopkins University. I'm following up on the study you were called about earlier."

"Oh, right. C'mon in." Freiberg stepped aside and held the door for Kaneko, who entered and took a quick look around. The room was simply furnished with a tan sofa, a few wooden chairs, and a couple of end tables. A single photo hung on the wall depicting a couple who Kaneko thought must be Freiberg's parents.

When he turned back to his host, he noted Freiberg taking a careful look around the neighborhood before closing the door. "Make yourself at home," the man said, and took one of the chairs for himself. "Strange thing to ask about, mathematics and the military."

"As with most things," Kaneko said, lowering himself onto the sofa and assuming his usual upright posture, "it is a matter of money. The competition for grants is intense. One of our administrators is hoping to expand the pool of available money. He thinks a demonstrated connection between the two might spur the Pentagon into making additional funds available for advanced mathematical research programs."

Freiberg laughed. "They'll throw money at anything that sounds good. It's hard to make materiel and boots on the ground sound sexy, but advanced math, yeah, that should do it."

Kaneko thought there was a bit of an edge in that response. "You don't approve of what we're doing," he said in a subdued voice.

"I don't care one way or the other. I did my hitch. I suppose somewhere along the line math can help defeat our enemies. But when you're over there in the thick of things, you know what it's about?"

Kaneko shook his head.

"Chaos. Terror. Blood. Not equations."

Freiberg fixed Kaneko with a stare that seemed to lower the room's temperature. The mathematician met it, hoping his thoughts weren't showing. He had never spent even a second in a war zone, but war was part of him. His home had been incinerated in a blinding flash, his father left to him as nothing but a story told by others. He thought he might in some way know more of war than this man who had walked through its midst.

"I gather you have some follow-up questions," Freiberg said.

"Yes." Kaneko opened the folder and took out his pen. "Did your mathematical background play any role in your options for military service?"

"No."

Kaneko noted the response on the paper. "Did your mathematical background afford you opportunities in the service that might not otherwise have been open to you?"

"No."

Another note, then, "Did you utilize your mathematical training while in the service?"

"Other than the same counting and adding that everyone else does? No."

"How about after leaving the service?"

Freiberg gazed at Kaneko for a moment, his face unreadable. "Why would you ask that?"

Kaneko shifted in his seat, suddenly worried. The question had been an intentional trap, one that he expected would only be sprung by someone who had something to hide. Otherwise, it should have received the same curt response as the preceding ones.

"What do you mean?"

Freiberg rose and walked to the window, looked around the neighborhood again, turned back to face the mathematician. "I thought you were interested in math and the military. Why ask about math and civilian life?"

Kaneko shrugged. "I didn't design the study. I'm just conducting interviews."

"I haven't worked since my discharge," Freiberg told him.

It wasn't an answer, Kaneko thought, but it was better not to press the matter. Freiberg's suspicions had already been raised, and that meant he had something to be suspicious of. He glanced furtively at the other and saw him watching as the response was noted down.

"Well, I think that will be all—" Kaneko was closing the folder when he felt a motion beside him and looked up to find that Freiberg had come to seat himself on the sofa. His gaze speared Kaneko. "Do you know what mathematical topic fascinates me most? Did you get that kind of information from my professors?"

Sarah's premonition leaped forth like an unsuspected predator. "We only have basic enrollment information," Kaneko said, fighting to keep the fear from his voice.

"Patterns. I love patterns. I seem to have a knack for them. Are you a mathematician or a social scientist?"

"A mathematician," Kaneko told him, then realized his mistake. He tried to squirm out of it by adding, "We don't have the funding to hire interviewers, so we have to do it ourselves."

"Money makes the world go 'round. I know. I had a bit of a problem with that myself, jobs being so hard to find. Good thing I had a cousin willing to help me out. But as I was saying—patterns fascinate me. They always have. I see them everywhere. When I was in high school I started seeing them even when they weren't really there. I saw so many of them that I worried I might have a mental illness. I had to get away from the numbers, so I joined up. Well, that and our country needed defending. The patterns followed me across the ocean and into combat, but that was a good thing. I could see what others couldn't. I could tell when someone who looked innocent wasn't." His eyes gazed on sights that Kaneko could not see, though he could well imagine the slaughter that filled them. "You can't imagine what that's like, the power of it, the terror of it, knowing that people live or die because you can see what they are through the patterns they're part of."

Freiberg stood. Kaneko took a shuddering breath. Freiberg strode to the window and stared out at the calm day. "When I came home, the patterns followed me back. But now they were different. I saw the life of terrorists in a cyclist, in an HVAC technician, in a family. I didn't know any of these people. They just happened to cross my path. They weren't really terrorists. I knew that. They were just people who happened to be parts of patterns over here that looked in some ways like patterns over there. But that made them useful."

He spun and crossed the room in three steps to tower over Kaneko, who had to press back into the cushions to see him. "Do you know what I'm talking about?"

Mute with fear, Kaneko shook his head. Somehow he had to get out.

But how?

"Actually, you do. It wasn't Peller, was it? He could never have figured it out. Not a Lucas sequence. But you could have, and you did."

Kaneko tried to scramble up, but as soon as his feet found the floor, Freiberg's fist smashed into his jaw. Fire engulfed his face to spread down his spine. He fell back heavily onto the couch, where the second blow caught him, shrouding his vision.

Σ

They glided in quietly, three detectives in one car and four uniformed officers in two squads converging on their quarry from opposite directions. At five minutes to two, the detectives arrived. "His car's gone," Montufar observed.

"Maybe he's gone to the store," Dumas suggested halfheartedly. All of them knew it was absurd.

Three minutes later the patrolmen arrived. Peller dispatched two to the back of the house and summoned the others to the front door with the detective team. Peller rang the bell and waited, but there was no response.

A moment later, Captain Morris called Peller to report that a search warrant had been issued for the property. "Looks like he's not here," he told her. "We should get Frey's license number and put out an APB on his car."

"I'll get on it," Morris replied and hung up.

Montufar rubbed her arms as though she were cold. "I don't like this."

"We might have expected it," Dumas told her. "If Rick's right that he plans to attack a big gathering, more likely than not that will take place in the evening."

"Then why isn't he here getting ready for it?" she persisted.

"Surveillance won't be easy," Peller said. "An out-of-place car would be too obvious and there's no good angle on the front of the place from the woods."

Dumas nodded across the street. "Maybe one of the neighbors would let us borrow a window."

"Have one of the officers check on it," Peller said. "And I'd better tell the captain we need that press conference." He began dialing.

"The sooner the better," Montufar agreed. Her companions occupied with their tasks, she retreated to the curb and perused the house. It was as nondescript as the surrounding houses; nothing outwardly sinister betrayed its occupant. Its silence taunted her. "Eric?" she called, and when Dumas turned she asked, "Have we heard from Professor Kaneko today?"

"The professor? I don't think so."

She looked at the house again. This time it made her think of brujos and poison toads. No, she didn't like this at all. Silently, and for the first time in more years than she could recall, she offered up a prayer.

Σ

Kaneko first became aware of his inability to move. It seemed his muscles refused to obey his commands as he tried to reach out, stretch his legs, roll over. The left side of his face throbbed with pain. He couldn't move his jaw any more than he could his legs. Panic washed over him and he struggled harder, until exhaustion overtook him.

Where am I?

He heard the sound of an engine, the rush of traffic. His eyes were open but he couldn't see anything, or at least no more than vague contours of lesser and greater darkness.

He remembered talking with Freiberg. He remembered coming to the realization that Freiberg was the killer the police had been calling Leo. Terrified, he had tried to get away, and Freiberg had hit him hard on the jaw. Nothing much registered after that, although he thought there might have been more to the struggle. Not much more, but more.

And now here he was, immobilized in the dark.

But where was *here?*

Experimentally, he tried moving one arm, then the other. His limbs, he realized, were indeed trying to move at his command, but were bound behind his back. The same had been done to his legs. A choking dryness in his mouth told him he had been gagged.

Freiberg had knocked him out, tied him up, and stuffed him into the trunk of his car.

What a cliché, he thought. He would have laughed at it if he could, but his throat was too dry for more than a croak.

But where was Leo taking him?

Imagination painted lurid possibilities. Kaneko forced them to the back of his mind, telling himself sternly that the main thing was that he was still alive. By all rights, Leo should have killed him, but something had stopped him, and the mathematician thought he knew what it was.

He didn't fit into Leo's pattern. His present situation was a curious repeat of the murder of the family of eight. The housekeeper hadn't been killed because her death would have disrupted the sequence. Whatever Leo was doing next, he couldn't kill Kaneko without interfering with the all-important pattern.

But Kaneko knew Freiberg's secret, too, so it was hard to see how Freiberg could let him live.

It didn't matter. Kaneko's objective was to stay alive as long as possible. An opportunity would present itself. Now that things had begun to go wrong for Freiberg, now that a crack had split open the neat little world he'd built around himself, opportunities would arise.

Σ

Freiberg had intended to arrive two hours early at the Columbia Holiday Inn—which, sited at the intersection of Maryland 175 and U.S. I, actually bore a Jessup address—check in, and prepare for the mission. The mathematician's arrival had thrown a monkey wrench into the works. He had a contingency for the possibility that Peller might be hot on his trail—one that involved going out in a blaze of glory—but he couldn't get this twist of fate to fit into any of the expected patterns.

As he drove eastward on route 175, carefully moving at the posted speed limit—much to the annoyance of many other drivers who wanted to exceed it by at least fifteen miles per hour—he pondered the implications. The mathematician must have been sent by Peller. At the very least, the police must have Freiberg on a list of suspects. When the mathematician failed to report back, they would know something had gone wrong. But was the little fellow specifically checking up on Freiberg, or had he been visiting multiple suspects? If the former, they would know who to look for. If the latter, they wouldn't be sure.

Either way, they would likely be looking for him, which meant he couldn't afford to be out in the open any longer than necessary. His car, in particular, was a problem. They could be watching for his license plate number. He'd have to ditch the car somewhere.

But that led back to the problem of the captive mathematician. Killing him outright would make a hash of the pattern, so that wasn't an option. Freiberg might make him a part of the operation this evening, but that entailed a lot of risk and would also alter the pattern, even if not as radically. Letting him go was, curiously enough, a viable option so long as it could be done without compromising the mission. That, though, was the problem. Freiberg couldn't have the mathematician running back to the police before the work was complete.

A considerable stand of woods bordered the rear of the Holiday Inn, separating it and nearby residences from Interstate 95. Freiberg had checked maps and scouted possible approaches through the woods when planning the operation. His original route seemed risky now, since it would leave the car too exposed and he wouldn't be able to liberate his prisoner without being seen. But given that the weather wasn't bad today—partly cloudy, temperature hovering in the upper 50's—he saw an alternative. He could leave the car in a less exposed area and stash the mathematician in the woods. If all went well, he would release him when the operation was complete. If not—well, he'd have to play that by ear.

But it still bothered him that the man was there at all. He couldn't make it fit into any reasonable pattern. What had Peller been thinking?

$$\sum$$

As a rule Captain Morris put considerable faith in her team. She paticularly trusted the triumvirate Peller-Montufar-Dumas. The talents of each contributed to a whole that was far greater than the sum of its parts. Rarely did she override them when they were all in agreement.

This, however, was one such time. The general who had accompanied Ralph Arriola to her office had already stressed to her the Pentagon's desire to avoid public disclosure should Leo turn out to be one of their own. The phrase "national security" had been on his lips almost as frequently as the word "the." Holding a press conference to ask for help in identifying gatherings of about one hundred people, particularly of military personnel, wasn't going to sit well with them.

Fortunately she had another idea, one she thought would succeed so long as she played it carefully. And quietly.

So after Peller's call, having only promised to make a decision on his request within the next hour, she closed her office door, extracted the business card that her military contact had left her, and dialed his number. She gave her name to the receptionist who answered, told her it was an extremely urgent matter, and in another fifteen seconds he was on the line.

"We have a name," she told him. "Luke Frey. Lives in Columbia, Maryland."

"Understood," he replied.

"There's more. We have reason to believe he's planning an attack on a gathering of about one hundred people, possibly today."

"I'll let you know if we find anything on him."

"You'd better do more than that. We think this may be a gathering of military personnel, something like a retirement party."

When no reply came, Morris continued, "We're talking about the lives of American soldiers. Your people are in grave danger. I need as much information as you can give me so we can stop him."

"There are national security interests at stake here," he told her, but he sounded less sure of himself than previously.

"I'm not your problem, sir. I know how to keep my mouth shut. But if this thing goes down as we fear, you'll have a PR nightmare on your hands. Help me to stop it."

After a moment, he said, "All right. I'll see what I can find and get back to you in half an hour."

Morris hung up and leaned back in her chair, exhausted. About damn time, she thought.

∑

The detectives broke in the door and dispersed to conduct the search. It was a small place: living room, kitchen, two bedrooms, one bathroom. Dumas started in what appeared to be Frey's room and Montufar searched the other bedroom. Peller did a preliminary sweep of the other rooms.

Dumas found the bedroom sparsely furnished and perfectly organized. The double bed was tightly made, the plain dresser contained neatly folded clothing, the closet contained more neatly organized clothing and little else. There was nothing under the bed, nothing hiding under or behind the clothing. Not even, Dumas thought wryly, any secret compartments or trapdoors.

Finished, he crossed the hall to see if Montufar had had any better luck and found her frowning into the closet. "Anything?" he asked, taking a quick look around. This room was a clone of the other. The identical furniture was even placed in the same positions relative to the door.

"No," she said. "The drawers are all empty. So's the closet. There's a panel in the back of the closet. I thought maybe something might be hidden behind it, but it's just access to the pipes behind the bathtub."

Dumas went to her side and looked. "Did you get down there and poke around?" Without waiting for her answer, he got on his hands and knees and took a closer look. "Nope. Nothing."

He was getting up just as Peller entered the room. "Nothing up front or in the kitchen. There's a laundry and utility room in back off the kitchen with an access to the attic."

"I'll go up," Dumas offered. "There's a ladder, I hope?"

"Yeah, back by the furnace."

They trooped to the utility room, where Dumas climbed up the ladder, lifted the access hatch, and poked his head into the darkness beyond. Peller handed a flashlight up to him and, feet still on the top rung, Dumas took a look around. The space ran the full length of the house with just enough room to stand beneath the ridge of the roof. It was unfinished, with insulation below and plywood above. A ten-by-ten area just around the access had been floored in plywood. A set of five large cardboard boxes lined the left edge of the floored area, and three more sat to the right.

"He's got something stored up here," Dumas called down. He climbed the rest of the way into the attic and investigated the five boxes to the left. They had been closed simply by folding the flaps together. Dumas opened them cautiously, only to be disappointed at their contents. "A lot of this looks like old clothes," he reported. "A few books. Stephen King, Dean Koontz. That kind of thing. Nothing unusual."

He crossed to the other three boxes and opened the first one. Within, he found a number of objects of varying size wrapped in white cloth. He picked up one and from the shape and weight of it knew instantly what it was. He unwrapped it, careful to keep it in the cloth.

He set it aside and lifted the next item from the box. It was longer and heavier, and the coldness of the metal within stole over him to envelop his whole body.

"Anything?" Peller called up, his voice impatient.

"Yes," Dumas replied, quickly looking into the other two boxes. Lying at the top of one of them was a nondescript three-ring binder; the sort of thing a fourth-grader might carry to school. He flipped it open.

He was staring at a checklist of the victims.

"What?" Peller said. "I can't hear you."

He returned to the hatch and looked down. Peller and Montufar stood directly below. "We got him," he told them, holding up the ten-gauge shotgun, still swathed in the middle to avoid fingerprinting it. "He's got a small armory up here. And that's just for starters."

∑

Alert for anything out of the ordinary, Freiberg turned onto Cedar Avenue and drove a quarter mile to its dead-end. No other cars were on the road and he saw nobody outside. So far, so good. The last three houses on the right stood across from Cedar-Villa Heights Park, and the paved footpath that looped around the park, offering access to its tennis and basketball courts, came out right at the end of the street.

Another glance around showed all to be quiet. Slowly, he drove his car along the path until he was hidden in the tall trees standing in the heart of the park. Several hundred feet back and around a curve, hidden from view from anyone not following the trail, he stopped, got out of the car, stretched, and casually scanned the woods once more.

All quiet. Good.

Freiberg silently opened the trunk and regarded the trussed-up mathematician. The man returned his stare, his eyes inscrutable. He didn't seem panicked, which was good. So long as he remained calm, he would be reasonably safe.

"I'm taking you out of the car now," Freiberg told him. He wrestled the mostly limp figure out and up onto his left shoulder, pressed the trunk lid down, and made his way into the woods. The trees here were dense; the undergrowth springing richly from damp soil and leaf mold. Counting his paces, he stopped when he thought he'd gone far enough, turned through three hundred sixty degrees to assure himself that he couldn't see anything other than trees, and set the mathematician on the ground, his back against a thick oak trunk.

The other squirmed a bit and tried to say something.

"Sorry. I can't have you yelling. The gag stays on for now." Freiberg checked the knots and, assured that everything was holding properly, stood. "I have to run an errand. I'm going to leave you here until I'm done. I should be back after sunset."

The mathematician made a sound that Freiberg thought was an objection. "Don't worry. I'm very good at finding my way around. I won't lose you."

He returned to his car, stopping just far enough back to be sure that nobody was around before emerging from the trees. He backed the car out the way he'd come, then turned from Cedar onto Lincoln Drive, which ran in front of the park. He left the vehicle in a parking lane there. He took a heavy duffel bag from the back seat of the car, locked up, and entered the park again, this time on foot.

It was about a quarter after three in the afternoon by the time he reached the woods behind the hotel. He took his time watching the parking lot, but at this time of day on a Thursday there wasn't much activity. He strolled out of the woods, meandered among the cars in the parking lot, and gradually made his way around the west side of the building to the main entrance. He checked in under his real name rather than the name he had given the police, and went up to his third-floor room.

Once there, he opened up his bag and extracted what he needed for the operation: a nice dark blue suit which he hung in the closet, a disassembled assault rifle, and two ammunition clips. He sat on the edge of the bed to check over the weapon.

He had three hours to kill.

Chapter 17

There are results and there are solutions. In some cases the result may be a proof that no solution exists. It occurred to me as I sat in the woods studying the trees and contemplating my fate that this might be a case in which neither solution nor discernable result existed. For no one can foresee the fallout from such events, and though the danger might be ended, certainly no one can claim that the questions raised by the matter have been solved. Σ

Captain Morris got her answers, although it took three times longer than the promised half hour. When her Pentagon contact called her back, the first thing he told her was that she'd gotten the name wrong. "It's not Luke Frey, it's Lucas Freiberg. Likely he gave you an alias, although why pick one so close to his real name? Makes no sense."

Morris jotted the name on a notepad. "What's the story on him?"

"I've been authorized to discuss that with you, but I have to warn you that this is classified information. You are not at liberty to disclose it to anyone except those within your department, and then only on a need-to-know basis."

"Understood," she said, impatience starting to get the better of her.

"Freiberg is an ex-Marine who was involved in some sensitive operations. Where doesn't concern you. He wasn't Special Ops. It's more like he operated in a gray area between what regular units and Special Ops units typically do. They say he had a real gift for telling the good guys from the bad guys. He was given a certain amount of leeway in utilizing that gift."

Morris jotted down notes as he spoke. "What do you mean, 'gift?'"

"He had a theory that there are patterns governing people's lives and that if you can see the pattern then you know what they're up to. It was uncanny how he could tell who was involved in operations against us and who was just an ordinary person going about his life. The point is, he was credited with taking out a fair number of insurgents, at first as part of organized operations based on his insight and later as something of a rogue operative. So long as he was right, the rules were allowed to bend to accommodate him."

"But then something bad happened."

"Yes. He murdered an entire family because, he said, they were the endpoint in a supply chain that delivered materials for IED's to insurgent forces. Some of them might actually have been, but he went in guns blazing and killed eight people, including several children. You can imagine the backlash."

Morris thought of the murdered family in Columbia. "How did you handle it?"

"Diplomatic assurances that justice would be served, financial payments made, and Freiberg shipped stateside pronto. Word was put out among the locals that he was facing a battery of charges and probable life imprisonment. In fact a deal was struck in which he would keep his head down and his mouth shut, and we'd give him a quiet but honorable discharge."

"A cover-up?"

"Compensation for the good he had done."

Morris wanted to say that whatever good he had done didn't excuse murder. She wanted to say that someone should have realized how unstable he was and at the least sent him for psychiatric evaluation. Instead, she asked, "Do you have his address?"

"He's got a place in Columbia," the other replied, and gave the address.

"We have people there now. With any luck it's already over and done with. I'll let you know when we have him in custody. What about a possible target?"

"There are no official functions taking place in Howard County in the next few weeks that would fit the bill. But retirement parties, birthday parties, that sort of thing—we wouldn't necessarily know about them. We aren't aware of any significant life events coming up for anyone associated with the incident."

After what she was sure were insincere thank-yous on both sides, she hung up and called Peller. When he told her they'd found a stash of weapons and ammunition, plus a binder filled with maps and notes related to the killings at Freiberg's house, but no sign of the man himself, whatever relief she'd been feeling turned to dread.

Σ

The dress Amber Janetta had selected for this evening was snug, with a bodice that plunged both front and back, made up from a satiny deep burgundy patterned with a lighter burgundy swirl. She had chosen it because it was the dress she'd been wearing the evening she and Master Sergeant Arturo Gutierrez met. He planned to propose to her tonight, a fact that she knew he didn't know she knew. He would think it an amazing coincidence that she wore this dress tonight of all nights.

The evening's event had been billed as Amber's birthday party. She turned twenty-eight today, and in typically lavish fashion Arturo was throwing her a bigger party than she would have wanted under most circumstances. But she certainly couldn't complain under these circumstances! He had rounded up about a hundred of their friends, nearby family, and military acquaintances to witness as he wished her happy birthday and then—surprise!—popped the question. He'd rented the biggest banquet room at the local Holiday Inn, opted for the priciest menu items, and ordered cake and champagne.

It's a good thing, she thought with a wry smile, that his family had money and was willing to foot the bill. She wasn't sure how they'd manage otherwise. His military pay and her receptionist's wages couldn't match strength with his extravagance.

She checked her lipstick in the mirror, blew her image a kiss, and picked up her purse just as he called from the living room, "Are you about ready?"

She strode out to meet him, and laughed with pleasure when his eyes light up like a pair of supernovae.

$$\Sigma$$

"A *notebook?*" said Montufar.

The weapons had been seized and sent to headquarters. Now the detectives dug through the binder, matching its contents to the killings. "A notebook," Dumas confirmed. "The first thing in it is a checklist."

Peller shook his head. "It's like the devil's book the Puritans used to talk about." A loose page fell from the notebook. "Map of Columbia. Look, there are places marked."

Carefully, using a closed pen, they turned the pages. "The sequences are here," Montufar murmured. "And it looks like he has a separate section for each of the victims—he was shadowing them two months ago. I wonder if any of them ever suspected."

"He was too careful," Peller said. "Too efficient."

"What would they have said?" Dumas added. "'I think someone's following me'? Would anyone have paid attention?"

"Probably just written it off as paranoia," Peller said, turning back to the beginning of the book. What Dumas had seen was revealed as a master list on which Freiberg had checked off each murder, as though inventorying a freezer.

Of the final and as yet unexecuted attack, however, there was no trace. "What do you think?" Dumas asked Peller.

"He must have made some record related to it. He's too meticulous not to. And this is his grand finale. Considering the amount of time and thought he put into his earlier victims—which, the way he thinks, would have been elementary exercises and rehearsals—he must really have spent some time working up this one. Let's get this to the evidence techs. Eric, you make another pass through the attic, and Corina, you recheck the rooms I already looked through. I'll search the bedrooms. Maybe one of us will see something the others missed."

After spending close to an hour examining everything in both rooms, Peller had uncovered nothing of interest. When he returned to the kitchen, he found Montufar seated at the table, a collection of paper scraps spread out on the table before her.

"Something?" he asked, hoping against hope for an affirmative.

"Maybe," she said doubtfully. "I was going through his recycling bin and found this stuff. It's an envelope, torn to shreds. I'm trying to piece it back together."

Dumas returned from the attic just as Peller sat down and looked over the scraps. "I hope that's not just a jigsaw puzzle," he said.

"Could just be a credit card offer," Montufar answered, "but I'm going to see if it turns into something worthwhile."

It only took the three of them a minute to fit it all together. It proved to be a plain white envelope with a first-class stamp in the upper right corner, hand-addressed to Freiberg. In the upper left corner was a sticker featuring an American flag, the name A. F. Gutierrez, and an address in Elkridge.

"No sign of the contents?" Peller asked, glancing back at the blue recycling bin.

"None," Montufar said.

"Did anybody notice the name while we were looking through that notebook?"

"Nope," Dumas said. "I'll get a number and call this Gutierrez."

Peller nodded and rose, returning to the table a moment later with the recycling bin. While Dumas moved into to the living room, cell phone in hand, Peller removed the contents of the bin and spread them out on the table. Mostly it consisted of boxes from frozen microwavable meals, newspapers, discarded junk mail, and a few window envelopes that probably had contained bills. "I shouldn't have missed those scraps," he said, irritated with himself.

"I almost didn't look at them myself," Montufar said. "Most of them were just blank chips of paper."

"Well, there's nothing here. What time is it?" He glanced toward the living room, where he could hear Dumas talking.

Montufar checked her cell phone. "Nearly five-thirty."

"Do you think we're missing something?"

She looked out the window at the dimming light. "Yes. But it might not be here to find. He might have taken it with him."

"And we have no way of knowing where he went." He nearly jumped when his phone rang.

It was Captain Morris. "I just got a call from Tom Kaneko's wife. She says he's gone missing. He was apparently playing a hunch based on some information he'd gathered on his own. You'll never guess who he went to see."

"Oh no. Freiberg?"

"Right the first time."

"But how did he know?"

"Long story. You might look for evidence that he was there, though."

Peller rushed to the living room with Montufar close on his heels, no doubt wondering what was going on now. Dumas was looking out the window, listening intently to whoever was on the line with him. Scrutinizing the furniture and the carpet, Peller shook his head. "We've been through this place thoroughly a couple of times. If he was here, he must have left again without leaving any clear traces."

Montufar stepped in front of him and mouthed, "Who?"

"Tom."

"My God."

Dumas said, "Thank you," snapped his phone shut and spun on his heel. "Whatever that is, it can wait," he told them. "We have to get to the Holiday Inn. Right now."

Σ

It was growing dark in the woods—dark and noticeably colder than it had been when Freiberg had left Kaneko bound and gagged by the tree. At first the mathematician had drifted in and out of consciousness. By now the pain in the left side of his face had dwindled to an incessant throb that he could sometimes ignore. Until he moved. Then it came hammering back.

Kaneko had been waiting a long time for Freiberg's return. He had no sense of how long, except that the sun had moved considerably, judging from the angle of the feeble sunlight diffusing through the leafless trees. He willed himself to concentrate. Three hundred sixty degrees in a circle. The earth rotated once every twenty-four hours. Thus it turned through fifteen degrees every hour. The angle from horizon to zenith was ninety degrees. How far had the sun moved? At a rough guess, a bit more than a half of that, a bit over forty-five degrees, a bit more than three times fifteen. He'd been alone in the woods for over three hours.

At least he was alive and not in immediate danger, but he foresaw two problems.

The first was, what might happen when Freiberg returned?

The second was, what might happen if Freiberg never returned?

It seemed to Kaneko that his best bet was to get away while he could. If he could. He couldn't move his arms or legs much, but he might be able to roll himself along the ground. Yes, that seemed likely. He could roll back the way they had come. There had been a road or a path or something there. Sooner or later someone would find him if he could get that far.

He took a deep breath and wrenched his body rightward. Bark caught at his hair and shirt as he crashed to the ground. Something sharp jabbed his face, probably deadfall from the tree, but he focused on the task at hand. Roll. His entire body screaming, he managed one rotation. Another. Over he went, slowly, painfully leaving behind the oak. Roll again.

Again.

So much pain.

Agony.

Endure.

Roll again.

He lay gasping on the floor of the darkening woods, staring up into the canopy. A breeze stirred the leaves.

He tried to roll again and failed.

Somewhere above and to his left, an extraordinarily bright star peeked at him through the leaves. *Kinsei*, he thought. *The metal star. It is here to give me strength.*

He tried to roll again.

$$\Sigma$$

At exactly five fifty-five, a well-dressed Lucas Freiberg picked up the duffel bag containing his assembled and loaded assault rifle, left his room, checked that the lock had engaged, and walked to the stairwell. He went down the stairs at a leisurely pace. On the first floor he strolled through the lobby to the wing housing the meeting and banquet rooms, where he located the venue for tonight's event.

He pulled his invitation from his suit coat pocket just in case, but nobody was at the door checking for them, so he went in. The room was filled with a dozen large round tables set for eight; at the front, a long table held room for ten. White table-cloths and burgundy runners draped the tables. The entire room smelled of roses. A few guests had already arrived and were chatting happily.

His invitation had indicated he would be seated at table four, which he found near the front of the room. He slid his duffel bag under his chair and sat, adopting a relaxed pose.

He watched people arrive, but he said nothing. He didn't know anyone here.

Not anyone who had shown up yet.

$$\Sigma$$

The sun was dipping below the western horizon with Venus shining brilliantly well above it as the detectives, with Montufar at the wheel and a red light flashing in the rear window, sped towards the hotel.

Peller called for backup and gave Captain Morris an update, then asked Dumas to fill them in on what he'd learned.

"This guy Gutierrez is a Marine. He's throwing a big birthday party for his girlfriend this evening."

"Did you talk to him?" Peller asked.

"They'd already left for the party. I talked to an uncle of hers. He has some medical issues and needs help getting around, so they have a couple of rooms at his place. He answered the phone and told me where they were going. Once I'd convinced him I really was a cop, that is."

"What's his connection to Freiberg?"

Tires squealed as Montufar took a sharp left.

Dumas hung on and waited for the g-forces to subside. "The uncle didn't know. But he verified that Gutierrez uses return address labels like the one on the envelope."

"A birthday party, presumably hosted by a friend," Peller mused. "It doesn't make sense."

"So what has made sense up to this point? Everything fits, at any rate. A big gathering, a military connection. The envelope must have held an invitation. Plus, he tossed the envelope but not the invitation, so presumably he'll be there."

They arrived moments later. Montufar whipped through the parking lot to the entrance and screeched to a halt. The three of them were out of the car almost before it stopped. Approaching the front desk, Peller flashed his badge at a pair of startled employees. "I need to see the manager right away."

The concierge began to stutter something. Montufar and Dumas headed for opposite ends of the lobby, checking down the hallways. Before the clerks could respond, a turbaned man dressed smartly in a gray three-piece suit came through a door at the left end of the desk. "How may I help you?" he asked calmly, glancing at the detectives and at Peller's badge.

"You have a birthday party scheduled here tonight," Peller said.

"Yes, the Gutierrez event." The manager's British-accented voice was cultured, as though he had been taught English by grandparents schooled under the Raj. "Is there some problem?"

"Very likely. We believe one of the guests may be armed and dangerous. We need you to keep the lobby and corridors clear. A number of officers should be arriving shortly. What's the layout of this place?"

The manager produced a map from beneath the counter. Peller imagined a bomb could go off next to the man without rattling his composure. "The party is here. From the lobby you'd go to the right and down this way." He traced the route with his finger. "There is access to the outside from here, and the kitchen staff will come in this way."

"I'll deploy the forces," Dumas said. Peller nodded his okay, and Dumas rushed out to meet the squad cars that were assembling swiftly and silently.

"Not to sound sexist," Peller told Montufar, "but you get back to the kitchen. Keep the staff out of that room and cover the door until the officers arrive."

"And you?"

"I'm going in."

"You sure that's a good idea?"

Peller grinned—rather wildly, Montufar thought. "No. But he made this a personal contest between us. It's just possible my presence might change things."

She squeezed his shoulder, then hurried toward the kitchen.

Peller looked at the manager and found him gazing back levelly. Peller thought that the man gave a whole new meaning to the expression "stiff upper lip". He looked positively serene. Somehow, Peller took comfort in the man's confidence. As he made for the banquet room, he thought that the Sikh gentleman was wasted on the Holiday Inn. He should be working for the Waldorf Astoria.

Σ

By six-twenty every table was fully occupied, except for the head table where the two middle chairs stood empty. A steady murmur of conversation filled the atmosphere. Off to one side, a DJ had set up his sound equipment and was playing tunes suited to the younger members of the gathering. The dance floor awaited the conclusion of the meal.

A curtain hung behind the head table, and behind the curtain Amber Janetta, bouncing nervously on the balls of her feet, held hands with Arturo Gutierrez. Gutierrez peeked around the edge of the curtain and motioned to the DJ, who cut off the song, switching to a jazzy rendition of "Happy Birthday." The couple stepped out from behind the curtain to thunderous applause and cheers.

Gutierrez helped Janetta into her seat, then held up a hand for silence.

"I want to thank you all for coming," he said. "My beautiful Amber turns twenty-eight today. We're going to make it a really special evening for her."

More cheering and applause followed his announcement. Janetta laughed and hid her face behind her hand in embarrassment. Then Gutierrez held up his hand again and silence fell once more.

"Now, all of you are family or friends of one or both of us. And a lot of you are in the military."

Someone in the back cheered and got a general laugh from the rest of the gathering.

"So I want to ask for a moment of silence to remember our troops around the world." He bowed his head and waited for about fifteen seconds before resuming, "Now, does anyone want to offer a toast to Amber before I do my own long, drawn -out, and badly rehearsed one?"

In the laughter that followed, someone called out, "We don't have anything but water to toast with!"

A look of confusion crossed Gutierrez's face as he realized the champagne he'd ordered wasn't on the tables. He looked toward the side door for some sign of the hotel staff, then noticed the man standing alert by the main doors, eyeing the tables near the front. *Who is that? I don't recognize him.*

A man stood up at table four. "I'd like to say something, Arturo. I think I can do it without alcohol."

Gutierrez, still confused, turned to face the man. "Luke? Well, hi, Luke! I'm glad you could make it. It's been awhile."

The man at the back began sidling toward the side of the room.

Who are you?

Gutierrez pointed to Freiberg. "Probably none of you knows Luke, Lucas Freiberg. We were in Iraq together. You got a toast for us, Luke?"

"Not precisely," Freiberg said. He bent down, pulled a duffel bag from under his chair, and slung it over his shoulder. The man from the door was behind him now, about fifteen feet back. He seemed to stiffen when Freiberg picked up the duffel, as though expecting to be seen.

"I wanted to apologize. What happened wasn't your fault, and certainly wasn't the fault of the rest of these good people. But you did play a role in it. Because of that, it has to end this way."

Clearly none of the unwitting partygoers had any clue as to what he was talking about, but Gutierrez did. A wave of panic poured through him. Freiberg cradled the duffel bag as though it were a weapon.

He has a gun. The knowledge flashed through Gutierrez's brain. *Did he plant an IED? We're all going to die.* "Luke," he said, dry-mouthed. "Don't do this. I'm not the enemy."

The newcomer behind Freiberg called sharply, "Put it down, Lucas."

Freiberg's face transformed into astonishment as he spun around. "Lieutenant Peller! Well, well. I was worried you weren't half as clever as I'd thought."

The bag and its contents were now trained on the man named Peller. A few people near the door took advantage of the distraction to slip out unnoticed by the gunman.

"It's over," Peller said. "There's no point in further..." He glanced around at the gathering. "Action."

"Of course there is," Freiberg told him. "This is the culmination, the point of the proof if you will. Until this is done, the result is not obtained."

"What result?"

"You don't know?"

Peller locked eyes with Freiberg. Gutierrez thought absurdly of rival sorcerers in a showdown. "It can't be that," Peller said at last. "It's too simple."

"Say it."

Peller shook his head. "You're much too complex for that, Lucas."

"Say it!" Freiberg screamed.

"You're just after attention?"

Freiberg made as if to throw the duffel bag to the floor, but maintained a firm grip on the strap nevertheless. "No! Not attention! Recognition!"

He spun about, shouting at the now-immobilized gathering. Even the music had gone silent, the DJ frozen in place behind his equipment. "If you knew what I'd done for you! If you only knew! I sold my soul to keep you safe! And what do I get in return?" His glare slid to Gutierrez's face. "Betrayal. That's what I get, Arturo. Betrayal! Betrayal at the hands not just of superiors, not just of fellow soldiers, but of friends. Of brothers."

Gutierrez saw that Peller was moving again, silently closing the gap between himself and Freiberg. "Luke, it doesn't have to be like this," Gutierrez risked saying. "Who has betrayed you? I wouldn't betray you. Not after everything we've been through."

"It doesn't matter anymore," Freiberg said. "Because after tonight, all wrongs will be righted. I don't expect to be alive to savor my victory, but I will have it."

Peller lunged at Freiberg, knocking him off his feet. Together they crashed onto his chair, which flipped and spilled them onto the floor. Freiberg was younger and stronger, but the duffel bag still wrapped around his arm pinioned him. Peller slammed his fist into Freiberg's face, but was thrown aside as the other twisted violently beneath him. He rolled away and started to come to his feet just in time to receive the full force of the duffel bag and its metallic contents on his left temple. He staggered, righted himself, and took another swing, but Freiberg slid out of the way.

A chaos of screams and trampling feet told Peller that the guests were abandoning the party. Out of the corner of his eye he saw the DJ dive from behind his table and scuttle across the floor to the exit.

And then the duffel bag was pointed at him like a weapon. "I can fire this whenever I'm ready," Freiberg said around gasps for air. Blood poured from his mouth.

"But you won't," Peller said confidently. "Not at me. I'm not part of your pattern."

Puzzlement creased Freiberg's face. "No. No, you're not. Thank you for reminding me."

He swung the bag around to train it on Amber Janneta.

"No!" Gutierrez bellowed, throwing his fiancée to the floor and covering her as a spray of automatic gunfire erupted, deafening Peller. For the first time Freiberg's shots were aimless, erratic, gouging holes in the walls and riddling the table linens as though his objective was to destroy everything, living or not. Any guests who had not already fled dropped beneath their tables or collapsed to play dead. At least Peller hoped they were playing dead, and hadn't actually been struck.

A resounding crack split the air. Freiberg dropped the duffel bag, stumbled, and crashed facedown to the floor.

His head ringing, Peller turned to see who had fired the final shot. Montufar stood just inside the doorway, a police sniper at her side. A dozen officers were behind her, the emergency medical team crowding close. He grinned weakly. "Good timing, Corina."

The silence was deathly. Peller couldn't tell how long it lasted. A pair of EMTs huddled over Freiberg's inert body while others checked on the guests and the crime scene unit photographers commenced their work. The remaining partygoers quietly gathered their belongings and dispersed. As he went out the door, one Marine, with a trembling blonde clinging desperately to his arm, called out, "Helluva party, Art. Can't wait to see what you do next year."

Chapter 18

The proverb says, "When you have completed ninety-five per-cent of your journey, you are only halfway there." By the end, I had acquired a new appreciation for that morsel of wisdom. $\sum$

Lucas Freiberg wasn't quite dead, but he didn't last long.

The EMTs determined that, miraculously, none of the partygoers had been injured. Then, while one of them checked on Peller's injuries, the others did their best to stabilize Frieberg and rolled him away to a waiting ambulance.

Montufar waded into the scene. "Rick, are you okay?"

"Yeah, I think so," he answered. At her look of concern he said, "I'm fine, Corina."

Dumas appeared as if by magic, asking the same question. Peller gave him the same answer.

The hotel manager entered and looked around at the demolished banquet room. "I've given all the guests a free room here tonight," he said, "for what it's worth. Perhaps it will help." He shook his head sorrowfully. "Such is the state of the world. Never in my days did I expect to see such a thing."

Peller didn't know what to say, but Montufar took the man's hand. "Thank you for all your help," she said sincerely. "Without you, it might have been worse."

He looked in her eyes for a moment, as a wise father might. "And without you, as well. Thank you, Sergeant." Then he returned to his office, calm as a cloud, and Peller wondered what he had seen in her.

Peller felt strangely detached, as if he had been dropped onto a movie set long after filming had ended. The crime scene unit buzzed about meaninglessly. A few feet away, Montufar and Dumas stood quietly speaking to one another.

One of the EMTs came up to him. "He wants to talk to you. Better hurry, though. I don't think he's going to last."

It was a strange request. Peller followed the woman to the ambulance.

His adversary lay on the gurney inside, pale as the sheet that covered him. IV and oxygen lines, along with other medical devices that Peller couldn't have named, crowded the space. He was careful not to bump anything. He wasn't sure whether he wanted Leo to live and face justice or simply die and rid the world of himself.

Freiberg was barely conscious, but he smiled weakly when he saw Peller's face leaning over him. "Good job," he said.

"Is this what you wanted?" Peller asked, unable to keep condemnation from his voice.

Freiberg shook his head once. It seemed all he could manage. "Soldiers don't *want* to die." After drawing a labored breath, he added, "But they know they might."

"Why did they deserve what you did to them? Patterson, Carrington, Lorna Bigelow? The Mason family, for God's sake? Why?"

"Collateral damage." His voice came so weak it almost sounded like he was falling asleep. "Part of the pattern. Ask the math guy."

Peller suddenly remembered the call from Kaneko's wife. Tom had gone missing after presumably talking to Freiberg. "Where is he?"

Freiberg's mouth moved, but no sound came out.

"Damn it, where *is* he?" Peller demanded, fighting the urge to grab Freiberg and shake him. The paramedic looked at him sharply.

"Safe," Freiberg said. Almost inaudibly, he repeated it: "Safe."

He said nothing more.

Σ

When Montufar went to tell Peller that Dumas had put out an alert on Tom Kaneko, she found him leaning against the side of the ambulance, staring at nothing. Not looking at him, she went to his side and leaned against the vehicle herself, watching the traffic on U.S. Route One, wondering what, if anything, he was seeing out there. Some minutes passed before Peller spoke.

"He's dead."

She nodded.

"We may never really know why he did it."

"Does it matter?"

Peller turned a puzzled look on her. "That's an odd question coming from you."

Montufar shrugged. "Our work is done. The shrinks can take it from here."

His eyes moving back to the traffic, Peller exhaled heavily. "There are a million more like him out there, Corina. A million. Gacy, Bundy, Dahmer, Leo. Kill one and another one rises to take his place. How many of them will end up on our turf?"

"God only knows," Montufar said. "Maybe there are too many shrinks in the world. Maybe what it needs is more shamans."

$$\Sigma$$

A gibbous moon had risen over the forest, providing just enough light for Kaneko to guess the distance to the edge of the trees. His whole body hurt and his vision was less than clear, but if he focused his mind he found it possible to estimate, from the motion of the moon and stars, that he had been working his way towards the road for nearly an hour and a half. It wouldn't be much longer, maybe another ten minutes of tortured rolling through the deadfall.

Somewhere nearby, a dog began to bark. It sounded close, perhaps from the road. Still gagged, he couldn't call out for help, but the sound spurred him on, and he struggled forward painfully, making another ten feet before stopping to gasp for air.

The dog continued to bark in a hysterical, high-pitched yap, as though it sensed the immediate end of the world. Now Kaneko thought he saw a light playing around the edge of the trees, and heard a woman's voice. He peered into the growing darkness. Yes, it was definitely a light, and its source was a human figure holding the leash of a tiny dog.

He forced himself to roll over a couple more times, making as much noise as possible.

The light found him, flashed by, then returned quickly to linger on his face. "Are you okay?" the woman asked tentatively. The light traced the form of his body, then returned to his face. "What happened to you?"

He squinted into the glare. The light moved out of his eyes, and once his pupils had adjusted again to the dark he saw a silver-haired woman gaping at him in horror while her white Chihuahua strained at the leash.

"You're tied up! Oh, Butterscotch, be still." The woman looked around in dismay, then tied the leash to a nearby branch. The dog continued to yap as its owner knelt by Kaneko's side. Are you okay?" the woman repeated.

Ignoring the gag, Kaneko tried to speak. All that came out was an otherworldly groaning.

Her fingers began working the knots. "Never mind; stupid question." The gag came off, and she started on the ropes. "Wait. Are you that missing professor? My husband heard about you on his scanner." Kaneko's hands came free. "He's a retired cop and likes to follow what's going on. Drives me crazy. Now he'll never get rid of it." The last rope fell away and she pulled out a cell phone. "The stupid thing's actually been useful," she said as she dialed.

Σ

As the crime scene activity was wrapping up, Eric Dumas, surrendering to impulse, found Corina Montufar and drew her aside. "Hey, Corina. Want to go out to dinner with me?"

She started to say no, she had other things to do—she needed to visit her brother at the hospital, there was a load of laundry to go into the wash—but unexpectedly found herself saying, "Sure. Where would you like to go?"

"How about that Chinese place?"

She laughed for the first time that day. "Only you would think to go there."

"They make a mean General Tso's chicken. What do you say—ten minutes?"

"Give me fifteen."

While they were eating, Peller called to tell them that Professor Kaneko had been found by a woman walking her dog. Leo's last victim would live to tell the tale.

After the bill had been paid, and Montufar was ready to beg off and head for the hospital, Dumas insisted on tagging along to meet her brother and wish him a speedy recovery. Eduardo was pleased to meet him—more than that, really; Montufar could have sworn that her brother was actually enthusiastic. But as she listened to the two of them speaking, she suddenly noticed that Dumas' laugh reminded her of Eduardo's—like a warm spring breeze that chases away the last lingering frost.

When she arrived home, she washed her clothes and threw them into the dryer, took a shower, and put on her oldest, warmest nightgown. She stood before the dresser for a long time, gazing at a framed picture of her family that she kept there. It was an old picture, showing her parents and much younger versions of Eduardo, herself, and Ella.

Then she opened a drawer she seldom used, and drew out her rosary.

Σ

The following afternoon, Peller went to the hospital to visit Kaneko. The professor's room overflowed with flowers: a large basket holding a brilliant mixture of roses, daisies, and forget-me-nots carried a card signed by Corina Montufar on behalf of the entire detective team; the mathematics department at Johns Hopkins had sent a smiley-face mug with a "Get Well Soon" balloon peeking over the top of yellow and white flowers; a smaller, simpler vase from the Holiday Inn staff carried a tasteful arrangement of lavender blooms. Peller instantly thought of a Purple Heart. Well, Kaneko deserved one, anyway.

The mathematician looked like a hospital patient: gowned and attached to an IV, his broken jaw wired, the wounds sustained while rolling out of the woods bandaged. Sarah sat beside him, knitting busily with a circular needle and a skein of blue yarn. She smiled when she saw Peller. "Hello, Detective Peller," she said. "Thank you for coming."

"Well," he said, feeling the thanks was completely unnecessary, "without your husband's help, we'd still be chasing a maniac."

She smiled again, and scooted her chair back so that Peller could talk with his unofficial assistant. Then she started in again on her project.

Kaneko opened his eyes. "You look ready to solve another case," Peller quipped. "Interested?"

Kaneko smiled. "I make a poor policeman."

"Well. You shouldn't have gone in without backup. But you did solve the case before we did."

"You were close behind. Thank goodness."

"Yes, but we owe you a debt of thanks."

Kaneko slowly closed his eyes and opened them again, as if his eyelids were performing the bow that the rest of him could not. After a moment, he said, "You look like you could use some time in the hospital, too."

With a smile, Peller said, "Probably, but I can't afford it. And anyway, as soon as the paperwork is done, I'm taking a vacation. I need to visit my son's family in Denver. It's been too long."

The mathematician smiled.

A knock at the door interrupted them. A nurse who to Peller's eye seemed young enough to still be a candy-striper entered, pushing a cart. "Hello, Professor. It's that time again," she said to Kaneko. "How are you feeling?"

He made a noncommittal sound.

The nurse fastened a blood pressure cuff around Kaneko's arm and ran a thermometer over his forehead. "You can have more pain medication at three o'clock," she said. "Ninety-eight point six. Looks good to me." She noted down the figures, then turned to Peller. "This guy is something else, you know that?"

Peller nodded. "Oh, yes. I certainly do," he said, meaning every word.

"Without him the police would still be chasing that lunatic." She shuddered. "He knew he could get killed, but took him on anyway. He's a good old-fashioned hero. We could use more like him." She straightened the covers around her patient. "Can you reach your call button? Okay. Just let me know if you need anything." She breezed back out the door.

There were a few moments of silence after she departed. Then Peller said, "I do have one question, though. How in the name of heaven did you get out of the woods tied up like that? I mean, I know you rolled the whole way. One of the doctors here told me in excruciating detail about what that did to your body." He winced at the thought. "But how could you actually do it? Most men, I imagine, would have given up almost at the outset."

Kaneko smiled carefully, as though gently probing the limits of his wounded face. "The mind," he said, "is stronger than the body. Every mathematician knows that."

Peller laughed.

And then he didn't.

Because, after all, it was the truth.

Q.E.D.

About the Author

Dale E. Lehman is a veteran software developer, amateur astronomer, and bonsai artist in training. With his wife Kathleen he owns and operates One Voice Press. They also have five chidren, four grandchildren, a laid-back Great Dane, and a couple of feisty cats.